TRIPLE CROWN

TRIPLE CROWN

Paul E. Patterson

5/'96

To alice— I will be interested
to know which incident stays
with you. I had a horse
run backwards and break
a hind leg, so I am partial
to that part of the story.

Paul Patterson

SUNSTONE
PRESS

SANTA FE

T he events, people, and incidents in this story are the sole product of the author's imagination. The story is fictional and any resemblance to individuals living or dead is purely coincidental.

Cover Illustration by Faith DeLong

First Edition

Printed and bound in the United States of America

10 9 8 7 6 5 4 3 2 1

Library of Congress Cataloging in Publication Data:
Patterson, Paul E., 1926–
    Triple Crown / by Paul E. Patterson.—1st ed.
        p. cm.
    ISBN: 0-86534-204-7
    1. Horse racing—New Mexico—Fiction. I. Title.
PS3566.A8238T75   1996
813' .54—dc20   95–44925
                                             CIP

Published by SUNSTONE PRESS
            Post Office Box 2321
            Santa Fe, NM 87504-2321 / USA
            (505) 988-4418 / *orders only* (800) 243-5644
            FAX (505) 988-1025

For Anndy,
my understanding wife, who spurred me on;
and Sheryl,
by horsey daughter, who advised.

1

Dock Trainham was an early
riser. This habit dated back to his youth when he had worked on ranches where cowboys sat down for breakfast at five. Over the past twenty-eight years as owner of his own spread he had still gone to the barn at break of day to milk and feed the livestock. The problem he faced now was how to pass the time while he waited for the motel restaurant to open at six.

He had rolled out from under the bedclothes in the Los Caballeros Motel this morning when the digital clock in the dark room showed a quarter to five. It had taken him about thirty minutes in the bathroom to shower, shave gray stubble off a weather-beaten face with a blade, pat on some after shave, and run a comb through a thinning patch of graying hair. He sat on the bed to slip off his bedroom slippers and pull on custom made boots while a beaming Willard Scott on the television screen talked about the weather.

With his hands braced on his knees, Dock turned to stare at the silent telephone on the nightstand. J.P. called at five-thirty, when he went to the cafe under the grandstand for coffee, to report on Paragon or any unusual happenings during the night at the track. Dock's wrist watch showed it to be twenty-five before six.

Impatience, goaded by the silence of the telephone, pushed Dock to his feet and set him to pacing around the room. Martha would say I'm stall walking, he thought. He stopped to draw back the curtains from the picture window overlooking the parking lot of the motel. Apache Peak, the alpine horizon that loomed west of the resort village of Sierra Vista, was basking in the rays of the rising sun. The pine covered slopes were emerald green and the granite pinnacle that topped the mountain like a dunce cap was as pink as a baby's cheeks. This mountainous vista always fascinated Dock who had spent most of his fifty-nine years on the monotonous grassy plains of West Texas. "I wonder what the hell's holding J.P." he muttered. He turned from the window and went over to sit on the edge of the bed. For something to do, he picked up yesterday's issue of POST TIME from beside the telephone to reread the article in the bottom left corner of the front page:

August 4, 1987, Sierra Vista Downs

Labor Day and the running of the Sierra Vista Rainbow Futurity when the top quarter horses in the country will vie for the pot of gold at the end of the race and the third jewel in the Triple Crown will be the climax of a summer season of racing here in the cool pines.

The running of the Texas Futurity last week found most of the handicappers tearing up their win tickets after Sonny Rogers rode Paragon of Merit, a long shot, through the opening on the rail to nose out Sun Shine, the favorite at 2 to 5 odds, to capture the first jewel. Literally the dark horse, Paragon, a black stallion, paid $42.50 to win.

Speculation and wild rumors about this long shot from West Texas are the topics of conversation as time draws near for the trial runs of the Oklahoma Futurity, and the second jewel. Was Paragon's performance a fluke or is the horse a natural? He ran a strong race and posted an impressive :21.46 pushing the two furlongs behind him on a fast track.

The two year old is owned by Dock Trainham from the Lazy DT Ranch at Horsehead Crossing, Texas. The trainer is track veteran J. P. Bates who returned to the winner's circle after several years absence. Paragon of Merit was sired by Wall Street and out of Wildcard, a little-known daughter of Mail Carrier. True aficionados who have done their homework in the history of the "Sport of Kings" will recognize that this newcomer carries a saddlebag full of genes for speed and heart.

Handicappers and touters alike will be hanging on the rail. . . .

The phone rang and Dock laid the paper aside and picked up the receiver. "Hello!" he barked.

"Mornin'," J.P.'s cheerful voice came from the other end of the line. "How you doin'?"

Dock breathed a sigh of relief. The call had come, and J:P.'s carefree tone seemed to say that everything was OK. "I'm fine," he replied. "How're things at the track?"

"Fine as rain," J.P. said. "Everything's jake here. Your horse took to that load of timothy hay you bought yesterday like a kid at the carnival takes to cotton candy. Cleaned out the feeder clean as a whistle. Tommy was graining him when I left for coffee. Reason I'm late phoning, I waited for Paragon to shit so I could check his droppings. The vet's tubin' did the trick. Not a sign of a worm; not even any eggs."

"Good," Dock said. "Did Tommy say everything was quiet last night?"

"Yeah," J.P. answered. "He kept Paragon on the walker for a little while after we left, then took him back to his stall. He did tell me that a couple of fellows he'd never seen before came by and spent some time looking Paragon over. But hell, that's not unusual. There's been a lot of interest and lookers since he win the Texas. Tommy said these fellows were dudes wearin' city clothes. You know, shoes, fancy pants, an' little narrow-brimmed cocksucker hats. Probably eastern tourists, figuring the way he described 'em. He said they hung around looking 'til he took the horse off the walker and headed back to the barn."

"They say anything to Tommy?" Dock asked.

"No, they just talked together, like they didn't want him to hear."

Dock did not comment for a few moments. "You know, that kind of thing worries me, J.P. I understand the curious lookers or those who just like to admire good horse flesh, but I'm concerned when I hear that some of these sharpies, these never-sweats who hang around the backside, are taking an interest in Paragon."

"Well," J.P. drawled in reflection, "Paragon upset a few people and a few well laid plans last week. Especially them that had a damned sight more than a two dollar ticket ridin' on the wrong horse. And Dock, you know there's big money invested on the nominees for the Oklahoma and Rainbow Futurities. Money that wasn't comfortable watching an unknown run the race Paragon ran. You can bet your boots there'll be a helluva lot of interest in his performance during tomorrow's qualifying race. If Paragon performs like you and I know he can, it'll be proof that he's more than a flash in the pan. He'll be recognized as a sure-enough threat an' your competitors are going to get a little nervous."

"J.P., you know that horse shit's not the only thing around the track that smells," Dock said. "I think we need to be takin' some precautions, what do you think?"

"We need to keep our eyes open, that's for sure," J.P. replied. "I think I'll put a cot in the tack room, and either Tommy or I'll bunk there at night."

"J.P., I think there should be one of us with the horse at all times," Dock said. "If it takes a cot and a thunder mug, plus some extra pay for Tommy to bunk there, that's what we'll do. You know if some sonuvabitch wanted to make sure we weren't going to qualify, it wouldn't take but a minute or two to doctor his feed or slip him a syringe full of those damned drugs that float around the barns. Do you agree with me or do you think I'm a greenhorn here at the track huntin' boogers and borrowing trouble?"

"Dock, you may be new to the racing game, and you may be huntin' boogers, like you say, but your concerns and precautions make good sense because there're damned sure some boogers out there. Runnin' horses on the track may be fun and games to some, but there's more than the glamour, trophies and winner's blanket at stake here. There're big bucks waitin' at the winner's circle. And Dock, it's a fact, not everyone plays the game according to Hoyle. With them, it's a no-holds-barred game of hard ball.

"Dock," J.P. continued, "your stud can run a hole in the wind. He's bred to run. He likes to run, and he's got heart. It bothers him to trail behind another horse. He's a natural with the disposition of a pussy cat. I'll tell you, Dock, I've seen lots of horses come and go in my day. Hell, I've sent my share of good ones across the finish line leadin' the field. But no bull shit about it, and I'm not telling you this just because you took a chance and gave me a break when I damned sure needed one, but because it's a fact. I don't know when I've seen a young horse that showed more promise than this black beauty.

"By God, Dock, it's sure as hell possible that Paragon of Merit might up and do the improbable. He just might win the Triple Crown."

2

Spending weeks on end in town was a new experience for Dock. He missed life on the ranch. Living, like he was, in a motel among all the young tourist families dressed in their summer play clothes left him feeling as out-of-place and solitary as a cow chip floating among the strawberries in a parlor punch bowl.

The waitress in the Los Caballeros dining room filled Dock's cup with steaming coffee and set the insulated carafe on the table. She took his order for two eggs over easy, biscuits, bacon, and hash browns. She told him it would be a few minutes before the order would be ready. The cook had come in late and the grill wasn't hot yet. Dock idly watched the few early customers drift into the sun-lit, large dining room with it's western motif but his mind dwelt on things at home. It's time to be thinking about contracting the calves, he thought. Thinking of how he should price the calves brought to mind that it had been just a year ago this week when Ross Malone was at the ranch contracting for fall delivery. He had priced last year's calves to Ross at two dollars above the market.

As he waited for his breakfast his thoughts drifted back to last year, Ross's visit, and the twist of fate that had him in Sierra Vista instead of at the ranch where he belonged. He and Ross had been sitting on the porch after a long hot day riding over the pastures in the pickup looking at the cattle. They were enjoying a tall bourbon cut with branch water and braced with a cool evening breeze blowing over Martha's rose bed. Four yearling colts were in a small trap fronting the house. Paunches full of summer grass, coupled with the coming of evening, had the young horses in a frisky mood. They were feigning fights, running and bucking around the small pasture.

Ross buttered his bread as a cattle broker. But his heart and soul, and most of his money to hear him tell it, were all tied up in horses he put on the tracks around the Southwest and in his speculative investments through the pari-mutuel windows. It was not long into the course of the conversation between the cowman and the trader when Dock found himself engaged in a one-sided discussion about cattle, the market, grass, and summer rains. Ross seemed to be lost in deep concentration as he stared out across the lawn.

"Let's step over and take a closer look at your colts," Ross said.

The two men stood bareheaded in the softening rays of the evening sun, leaning their forearms on the top rail of the yard fence, watching the gamboling horses. After a long study, Ross broke the silence: "Dock, tell me about that black stud colt. Is he out of one of your ranch mares or did you buy him?"

"Well sir, I'll tell you the story," Dock said. "I was in El Paso at a horse sale, hunting for a stud. Early on in the course of the auction they ran a hard-looking old mare into the ring. A couple of things about the old mockey caught my attention. In a world of bays and sorrels, here was a solid black mare. The announcement by the auctioneer said she was a registered Quarter Horse, a daughter of Mail Carrier.

"The name Mail Carrier rang a bell in my memory. While the auctioneer was trying to raise an opening bid on the mare, I got to thinking about where I'd heard or read about that stud. Then it came to me: several years ago, during a bull-buying trip to California, Martha and I had gone to the horse races at the Alameda County Fair Grounds. We'd watched this horse Mail Carrier sweep a race. Ross, you know I'm not a hand to follow track horses, I'm a cuttin' horse man. But that race and Mail Carrier left an indelible impression on me. That damned horse left the starting gate like he had a bobcat riding on his croup, and he never let up. When he crossed the finish line, he was an easy six lengths ahead of the nearest horse and was lengthening his lead with every stride. I remember telling Martha that the horse was well named because he sure enough had carried the mail, from the start to the finish. Then, later that same year, I read that the horse had to be retired from the track because of an injury.

"Well, I watched as the ringman moved the old mare around the ring," Dock continued. "She'd sure been on slim pickin's. She hadn't even started to shed her winter coat and her hooves showed she'd been foundered. She was as poor as a town dog. The auctioneer started her at a thousand."

Dock took a drink from his bourbon and water, then continued his story: "The auctioneer wasn't having any luck so he dropped the asking price to seven-fifty. He granted to the crowd that the old mare looked a bit rough, but he pointed out that she was a diamond in the rough. He kept crying that she was an own daughter of Mail Carrier, a purebred, proven runner, and that her dam was permanently registered in the Quarter Horse Association.

"The auctioneer still wasn't getting anywhere. Everybody was bull shittin', and not paying any attention. He dropped the price to six and sweetened the pot by announcing that the mare came with a vet's certificate showing her safe in foal to Wall Street, a registered Thoroughbred that had set track records that still stood. The crowd sat on their hands, so he banged his gavel on the table and asked for five.

"I was wishing that the ole mockey would look somewhere besides at me with those sad, sunken eyes. Somebody had to take her home or she'd go to the killer for dog food. She whinnied and pawed at the sawdust floor covering like she knew she was in trouble. Looking at her I figured it would take a truck load of feed to put her in condition to raise a colt, that is if she didn't abort it. But then on the other hand, I reasoned her sire was sure some kind of runnin' horse and even though she looked like crow bait now she musta been a helluva mare in her day. She girted big, had a good straight leg standing under each corner, an intelligent look in her eyes, a straight back and a good slope to her croup.

"Ross," Dock continued, "I sure didn't need that mare, but she was in foal to Wall Street, a full brother to the old foundation sire Traveler. Her breeding, coupled with Wall Street's, was hard to ignore. I got to thinking: If I could get a live colt out of her, I might have something. It might be a horse colt that I could use as an outcross on my mares. The auctioneer was still hammerin' on five and threatened to pass her out. I waved my hand."

The colts came up to the fence to stick their necks out for a cautious smell of Dock's extended hand. "Martha came out to meet me when I drove into the yard," Dock said. "I backed the new stallion out of the trailer first, hoping she'd be so impressed with him that she wouldn't ask about the hard-looking mare I'd bought. She didn't hardly see the stud, she couldn't see anything but that starved-out mare. Talk about mad, she bristled up like a dog on the fight when she saw how someone had abused the old girl. By God, Ross, there for awhile I didn't know if the mare was going to take up residency in the house with us, or if Martha was going to move our bed out to the barn."

The sun had slipped below the horizon and the cool evening air was dispelling the August heat of West Texas. The colts had gone to the back side of the pasture and Dock and Ross's bourbon glasses were empty so the two turned and headed for the house. As they walked across the yard, Dock continued with his story: "The mare foaled in the summer, a catch-colt, solid black like his mamma. I was going to name him Lágrimas after a black stallion in one of Tom Lea's books, but Martha had other ideas. She wanted to call him Paragon of Merit. I argued that it was a pretty high-falutin' handle for a cowpuncher's horse. But as you might guess, the colt's registered name is Paragon of Merit.

"Well sir, I floated the ole mare's teeth, wormed her and loaded her up on vitamins. Nothing would satisfy Martha short of ordering a load of timothy hay from way up in Colorado. As you know, Ross, Martha won't weigh a hundred pounds soakin' wet, and she's a good-natured woman; but when she finds a cause, she'll champion it like she was fighting a swarm of bees. That old, abused, pregnant mare provided her with a cause."

The friendly young waitress broke into Dock's reverie when she sat a plate in front of him. "Here's your breakfast, Mister Trainham," she said. "I'm sorry it took so long. I'll bring you some more coffee."

Dock diced the eggs, split a biscuit and buttered it. Paragon had caught Ross's eye and Ross had a reputation of being a good judge of horseflesh. But hell, anybody with an eye for a good horse would have taken a second look at Paragon, Dock recalled as he worked at getting around the plate of bacon and eggs.

Dock had noticed the yearling showing signs of developing into a horse built for speed. From his dam, Paragon had the wide spring of ribs and deep barrel of a quarter horse, coupled with the length of body and clean legginess of his thoroughbred sire. Racing around the pasture, Paragon seemed to float effortlessly over the ground, his well-coordinated, long, smooth muscles rippling under the sleek black hide. And as Ross pointed out as they had watched the colts running and playing, Paragon not only showed the reach and long stride of an early foot, but he ran as a born leader of the field, not a follower. "He looks to be a natural for the track," Ross said.

While Dock had worked at preparing supper, Ross had done some figuring at the kitchen table with his pocket calculator. He agreed to take the calves at Dock's price and pay market price on the day of delivery for the cull cows and bulls. They agreed that Ross could cut any unmerchantable, Dock would have the cattle ready for an early morning delivery in mid-October, and that they would shrink the scale weight by the customary three percent. The problem arose when Ross asked Dock to throw in, as boot, the black colt.

Dock had not commented, but thought about the trade as he fixed Martha's plate and carried it into the bedroom to her. While he fixed her pillows, helped her to sit up, and set the tray across her lap they talked about the day's happenings. She asked how Ross had liked the calves and if Dock thought he had them sold. It was as Dock turned to leave that she asked how Paragon

14

was doing. That was the deciding factor.

Over supper Dock told Ross that he appreciated the offer on the cattle, but if it took the colt to make the trade, there would be no deal. Ross had argued, pointing out that he was offering top price for the cattle. When Dock stood pat, Ross countered by saying he would take the cattle as they had agreed, and give three thousand for the colt.

In a hesitant voice, Dock told Ross that as he had told him that morning when Martha didn't come out to say hello, she was under the weather. But what he hadn't told him, was that Martha was bedridden with leukemia.

"Ross, the colt's not for sale," Dock said. He went on to explain how Martha had helped the old mare raise the colt by bottle feeding it, and how it had given them something to talk about beside Martha's failing health. He talked about the fact that the only pleasure Martha had was when he would lift her out of bed, put her in a wheel chair and push her out on the porch so she could watch Paragon run and play. "Sometimes," Dock said, "if she's feeling strong enough, I'll wheel her out in the yard and lead the colt in to where she can pet him."

Ross said that he was sorry to hear about Martha. Several minutes passed as the two men seemed to concentrate on eating. Ross broke the silence when he looked across the table at Dock and said: "If the cattle trade stands, will you agree to give me first refusal on the colt?"

Dock studied for awhile before he replied, "I don't know, Ross. He shows the making of a good saddle horse, got a good disposition and he's sensible; or like I said this afternoon, he might make a damned good replacement stallion. Being Martha's pet like he is, well, I've never thought anything about what I'd do with him down the road. We just try to handle one day at a time around here.

"One thing's for sure," Dock added. "As long as Martha's alive, I won't move the colt from where he's at. Not while she can see him an'...." Dock pushed up from his chair and went to the stove to bring the coffee pot to the table.

"Dock," Ross said, "you know I've agreed to pay top dollar for your cattle. I damned sure haven't paid as much for any of the other cattle I've contracted for this fall. You don't feel like you can help the deal by throwing in a yearling colt. Well, I guess I can understand your position, considering Martha, and all. I'll tell you what I'll do. I've made my offer on the cattle and I'll stand by it. I will also give you a check now for three thousand and I want you to give me an open-dated bill of sale on the colt. You keep him here at the ranch for as long as you need him, up to a year. Don't do anything but halter break him. Don't castrate him and don't brand him."

Dock studied the set look on Ross's face. Martha's colt had become an issue of contention in what should have been a deal involving only the cattle. The horse itself isn't the issue, Dock thought as he wrestled with the problem. Horses come and go, and considering the premium Ross had offered on the cattle, the yearling colt would be well sold. Maybe I look at Paragon as being Martha's, or maybe it's the idea that I don't like being pressured after I've said no, and given what I think is a pretty good reason for it, Dock thought. He could feel the tension rising in the back of his neck and his face flush as he gave way to rising anger.

"Ross," he said slowly, "the horse isn't going to be any part of the trade. Now, if you want out of the cattle deal, that'll be fine. Cattle buyers are like buses in El Paso, there's one along every fifteen minutes."

Ross made no immediate reply. His florid face flushed and his eyes hardened. He pulled a pack of cigarettes from his shirt pocket, shook one out, and lit it. After several deep pulls on the cigarette he exhaled slowly and the color drained from his features. "My offer on the cattle stands," he said, "and as you know from our past trades, I don't welch on a deal. But I'm going to give you some boot, some advice. I know you're not interested in the business of racing horses, so listen to what I've got to say. As a man who only uses a horse to push a cow around or prowl a pasture, and don't know shit from apple butter about racing pedigrees, you stepped into a pile of horse shit when you bought that old broken-down mare and walked out of it smelling like a rose.

"You ended up with a stud colt carrying a strong pedigree and showing definite signs of early foot. A natural that a man doesn't chance onto every day. You see the way that colt handles himself?" Ross asked. "He keeps the pieces neatly tied together, and hell, he's still in the growing, awkward stage. Do you notice how he can't stand to be behind the other horses when they're running? Yeah, you recognized some merit in his pedigree when you bought the mare and figured you might get a decent saddle horse or stud for your mares, but shit, you probably don't have a clue as to how strong that pedigree is.

"My advice to you," Ross continued as he snuffed out his cigarette in his plate, "don't turn that horse into a ranch gelding. Take him to a good trainer before he's two. Give the horse time and the training it'll take for him to grow into his potential.

"I'll recommend a fellow named J.P. Bates as a trainer. You'll hear about him and wonder why the hell I would recommend him. He's had a run of bad luck and he's got a drinking problem, like some of the rest of us race track bums. But he's damned sure a good horseman. Probably the most gifted man with a horse that I know, and he sure as hell knows the racing game. He's down now, but take my word about his abilities. Go talk to him. You'll find him hanging around Sunland Park or Sierra Vista Downs."

Ross pushed his chair away from the table and stood up. "I'll call you when I get a date set for the cattle truck," he said as he started for the back door.

"Where you going?" Dock asked.

"To town," Ross replied as he took his Stetson from the mounted deer horns that served as a hat rack by the kitchen door.

"The sun's down and it's a long drive to town," Dock said. "Don't you want to bed down here for the night?"

"I got lights on my car," Ross snapped. He paused at the door and said over his shoulder: "Trainham, I want you to remember that if I hadn't told you what you've got in that horse, you'd have no doubt made a saddle horse out of him, and you can buy a damned good, broke saddle horse for the price I've offered you. I'll wait, but by rights, I want my offer for first refusal. Don't forget."

Thinking back about Ross, the old mare, and the naming of Paragon of Merit had turned Dock's thoughts to Martha. On his drive to the track after breakfast Dock thought back over their marriage, their years together and how his greatest pleasures had been in making her happy and to be on the receiving end of her show of appreciation and affection. "She was a loving, kind woman, a good wife and a great friend," he said to the steering wheel.

In all of their twenty-four years of marriage there had been only one difference of opinion which they could not resolve. That was how best to raise Martha's boy, Patrick. She thought Dock was too hard on him. Once, in a rare spat, she had confronted Dock with the accusation that he would not be as strict with Patrick if he were his own flesh and blood instead of an adopted son. Dock had denied this but sometimes, inwardly, he wondered if she might be right. However, he reflected, in that little flare-up of tempers he should have bridled his tongue. In the heat of the argument he had retorted, accusing Martha of being overly protective, of mollycoddling Patrick. He told her she was making a mamma's boy out of him. Dock chuckled to himself as he recalled her reply: "Mr. Trainham!" she had flared, "you can damned well go sleep in the bunkhouse. Our bed's not big enough for the two of us."

"She could be pretty feisty if you got her on the prod," he mused.

Dock had been a bachelor in his mid-thirties when he met Martha, a divorcee with a child from a previous marriage. During their courtship they had discussed the matter of adoption. Dock had said that he would like to have the boy carry on the Trainham name. To celebrate their first wedding anniversary Martha had given her consent, and Dock adopted Patrick. Dock willingly shouldered the responsibility of being a father. But he found that he preferred the sound of a calf bawling for it's mother to the crying of his son, and the smell of horse and cow manure to that of soiled diapers in the house. He was happy to leave the raising of Patrick to Martha.

Martha, so desirous for a happy union after the heartbreak and soul-scarring trauma of an unhappy marriage and bitter divorce, tried to shield the marriage and Dock, who was set in the ways of bachelorhood, from the problems of raising a child. Rather than have a family confrontation over disciplinary matters, she would privately plead and cajole with Patrick, trying to get him to mind. Most often, however, she let the boy run on a loose rein.

3

Paragon of Merit was scheduled

to compete in a qualifying race for the Oklahoma Futurity on Tuesday morning at eleven thirty. Dock reported at the racing secretary's office on Monday. He exchanged pleasantries with the filing clerk, an attractive brunette wearing a form-fitting shirt. He handed her the health certificate from the veterinarian, pulled a pen from his shirt pocket and put his signature on the stack of forms she set before him.

It's a damned shame a man has to get long in the tooth and leave all these good looking women to the young bucks, Dock thought to himself. He smiled and took one last glance at the tight-fitting Levis covering swaying hips and a petite posterior as the girl walked away from the counter. He chuckled as he thought how Martha used to tell him that it was all right for him to look but to remember that he had more waiting for him at home than he could handle. He left the office and headed out into the early morning sunlight. He had told J.P. he would meet him for coffee.

The Canter Inn, on the ground level under the grandstand, was crowded with trainers, grooms and owners taking their morning break after their charges had been taken care of. J.P. was engrossed in the Daily Racing Form and had a cigarette burning in the ash tray in front of him. From his scuffed boots to his sweat-stained western hat he fit in with these backside track people like a Coke bottle fits with Coke bottles. The short order cafe was abuzz with talk and heavy with tobacco smoke and the pungent odors of grease and simmering chili. Flies buzzed at the windows and around the tables, or they blackened yellow spirals of fly paper streamers hung from the window frames.

A harried waitress swiped a damp rag over the red and white table covering and filled two porcelain mugs with coffee. J.P. frowned as he took a cautious sip of the steaming black brew, put his cup down and said: "I've been looking over the performance of the Overton filly. She's going to be the one to beat Thursday, and I'm not sure we can outrun her. She's already posted some damned good times. I've seen her and watched her run. She's got a powerful rear end, good action and a helluva stride. If Paragon gets a clean break from the gate I'm certain he can post a qualifying time, even if he doesn't break the wire."

"He's been handlin' good at the gate," Dock said. "I don't think he'll have any trouble there, do you?"

"Well," J.P. drawled, "on a short straightaway, a helluva lot can happen comin' out of that gate." He took another sip of coffee, then glanced to his right and to his left over his shoulders. Satisfied that no one was paying any attention to them, he pushed his hat to the back of his head, leaned into the table toward Dock and continued in a confidential tone: "Things happen at the starting gate that can influence the outcome of a race, especially at two furlongs. Some are just breaks of the game, like if a horse isn't ready, you know, not standing on all fours, or gets a bumped start when the gate opens. But there're some poor starts that aren't accidents, or not the horse's fault. Winning's the name of the game and some trainers and owners aren't above greasing the right palms in order to win, or even lose if it suits them. Believe me, there're jockeys, gate handlers, and even vets who aren't above lining their pockets with easy money."

A frown creased Dock's face as he studied his coffee cup, digesting J. P.'s statement. Finally, he looked up and said: "I can figure how a race can be jimmied, but I don't see how a horse can be slowed down coming out of the starting gate without some deliberate action by the jockey or the handler that would be obvious."

"Stop and think about it," J.P. responded as he ground out the butt of his cigarette in the ash tray. "The horses are led into the starting gate. They've been there before and know what's about to take place. Most of 'em are keyed up. They're nervous and edgy, you know, like a ropin' or doggin' horse in the box. That's why gate handlers stand in the gates by the head of each horse, holdin' onto a rein. That way the handler controls the horse. He keeps it from rearin', or gettin' it's head down between it's knees. It's their job to hold all the horses at the ready. But at the sound of the starting bell a sudden flick of the handler's wrist and a tug on the bits, or any disturbing movement as the gates open can distract the horse and make for a poor start. Hell, Dock, I know a gateman who wears a big diamond ring. He'll get the sun's reflection flashing off that diamond into the horse's eye. Of course the horse is bothered. It gets to throwing it's head, or battin' it's eye, trying to get away from that blindin' light. Works damned near every time. Hell, any little thing to distract the

20

horse at that critical moment can make it break slow. Most two furlong races are run in less than twenty-five seconds, so you can figure what the loss of a second or two can mean in the outcome. There's hardly time to overcome it. There are ways and means, Dock, and people who break the rules are pretty cagey with their little shenanigans."

Dock sat back in his chair. He glanced around the room full of coffee drinkers. The trainers, jockeys, veterinarians, farriers, stable hands; the people who were behind the scene in the racing industry. Leaning back over the table he said to J.P. in a guarded voice: "Everybody hears stories about fixed races, and I'm sure some of that goes on. I'm just a shit-kickin' cowboy from the sticks, green as a gourd about the facts of life on the track and backside, but I would hate to think that jockeyin' the outcome of races is commonplace. That would be like me playing poker against a marked deck. Only on the track the sucker is the bettor who's laying down his money on a hunch or what he thinks he knows about the horse's abilities to run after he studies the dope sheets."

"Dock, bettin' the horses is no different from anything else where there's big money at stake," J.P. said. "If you're gonna play poker for big stakes you better know who you're playin' against. At the track the stewards and the racing commissioners hold a tight rein and most races are run straight. But you'd still better know who you're runnin' against 'cause it's a fact of life that there are races that are run in motel rooms or behind closed stable doors before the bugler ever blows post time. "Well, anyway," J.P. said as he cinched his hat down on his brow and shoved his chair backward, "we'd better head for the barn. Time's gettin' short and there's something I want to discuss with you, but I don't want to do it here."

Dock laid a dollar bill and three quarters on the table. They headed up the graveled roadway toward the barns. As they walked along, J.P. talked: "I want to tell Sonny to push for second or third position by the half-way marker in Thursday's race. Then, if it's a tight race, he's to go to the bat if he has to hold his place. If he feels Paragon driving to pull ahead, I'll tell him to ease back and coast along behind the leader. I'm sure that'll assure us of a qualifying time."

"You're talking about telling Sonny to rein in if he has to. Is that in accordance with the rules, J.P.?"

"Well, not exactly, the rules state that any instructions to a jockey, other than for the purpose of winning, are a violation. But...."

"Wait a minute," Dock interrupted. "If it's breaking the rules, then why are we even discussing it? We just got through talking about the sorry business of fixing races, now here we are, plotting to do just that."

"Dock, I'm not talking about fixing a race, I'm talking about planning strategy. There's a helluva lot of difference."

"What the hell's the difference between fixing a race and what you call strategy?" Dock retorted.

"Dock," J.P. said in a restrained voice, "we may be worrying over nothing. Paragon might have to run his heart out to even qualify. All I'm suggesting is that if it comes easy for him, let's just ease up and keep our ace in the hole. Sonny's got good hands, light when they're needed, and he's no novice. He'll understand what we want. Jockeys realize that if they want the mounts, they take instructions from the trainers and owners on how to handle the horse and run the race. They know how to keep their mouths shut too. Otherwise they won't find mounts. Sonny knows Paragon. He'll ease onto the bit if he needs to, and it won't be obvious."

"I still don't understand your thinking," Dock remonstrated. "Why don't we just let the horse run his own race?"

"I think maybe Paragon can win, or at least place in the money. That's what concerns me," J.P. said. "Look Dock, you own the horse and I'm just a hired hand, but if you want my opinion I think you should be considering more than just posting a qualifying time on Thursday. For the long run you need to be thinkin' about the upcoming Oklahoma and Rainbow Futurities and the odds on Paragon when the betting windows close on those big money days.

"You've got yourself a strong contender in that black horse," J.P. continued. "One the handicappers or the smart money boys haven't gotten a handle on yet. If you play your cards right you can parlay that in several ways. Don't let anybody see your hole card for the Oklahoma until the bets are down. That way, if you feel confident you can take advantage of Paragon's long odds and lay some bets down yourself. You know your horse and it's capabilities. If you don't underestimate the competition you stand a damned good chance of not only winning part of the purse, but also hitting the pari-mutuel for a bundle."

"J.P., if Sonny has to rein in Paragon to finish where you want him to and gets caught at it, I'm in trouble with the stewards. I've spent a good bit of money and time getting that horse to this point. Money and time I don't have to throw away. I sure as hell don't want to get called on the carpet for violating the rules and get fined, or have Paragon scratched."

The jaw muscles under J.P.'s ruddy cheeks bunched as he clenched his teeth. His normal somber look darkened with the rise of his Irish temper. He looked away from his employer, out over the expanse of grassy turf in the heart of the oval track. He seemed to concentrate on the three banners hanging limply from the tops of flag poles beside the tote board. The risen flush ebbed from his features as he slowly bridled his temper.

"That's fine with me," he said in a tight voice. "As you damned well know, I lost my license once by thinking I was too smart to get caught breaking the rules. That stupidity cost me my family and five long years of wasted life. This runnin' horses isn't just prestige and a test of horseflesh. For most, it's a scramble for the almighty dollar. I only got one thing standin' between me and the soup kitchen and that's my ability to train horses. I'm a damned good trainer. I know horses and I know racing. I'll guarantee you I'm not going to take any chances on getting suspended again. Not for you. Not for any son-of-a-bitch. You're inferring that I'd be stupid enough to jeopardize my license. No way, man. I'm playin' it straight and keeping my nose to the grindstone. Trainham, for me the track is not just some feather-up-the-ass pastime like it is for some people. It's my livelihood and the means to gettin' my family back."

Dock stood where they had stopped, his hands thrust deep into his pockets as he listened to the normally closed-mouth J.P.'s tirade. The trainer's hardened, flushed features and the narrowing of his eyes were a study in the effect of an internal struggle. After J.P. fell silent, Dock pursed his lips, and after some moments in thought said in a constrained voice: "J.P., I've seen some of these boys pulling their mounts up during a race. I don't want to be a part of that. If you want to train for me, we'll abide by the rules, and Paragon will run his races straight."

"You got it," J.P. said and headed for the barn.

4

Sierra Vista Downs lies in a spacious valley beside an arterial highway leading to the resort village. It's a sprawling complex of barns, horse stalls and parking lots. A two-tiered covered grandstand and a picturesque track arena are carpeted with Kentucky Bluegrass surrounding a turquoise lake. The racing season gets off to a running start on Memorial Day. The tempo builds during the summer months to climax on Labor Day with the running of the Sierra Vista Rainbow Futurity. The top registered Quarter Horses in the nation compete for the two million dollar jackpot purse that waits at the finish line of the two furlong futurity.

The challenge of selecting and wagering money on the three horses that will run in the money, enhanced by the beauty and freshness of summer under the cool pines, attracts sporting vacationers, horsemen, track employees, racing aficionados, hard-core gamblers, con-men, drug dealers, prostitutes and mobsters.

It may be, as the old track-wise bettors claim, that it's the housewife who buys a two dollar show ticket on the favorite that supports the racing industry. But it is the pie in the sky chance of parlaying a two dollar ticket into a bundle that draws the crowds on race days to the ground-level stand where the general-admission bettors drink beer from paper cups and flock to the track railing to urge on their picks. In the upper tier, the Jockey Club patrons sit in their boxes, laying their bets in multiples of hundred dollar bills, while attractive young ladies in designer jeans serve Crown Royal and hors d'oeuvres.

The grandeur of the Sport of Kings on a day of racing surrounded J.P. as he readied Paragon for the Oklahoma Futurity trial run. The barn area was alive with horsemen and horsewomen attending to their sleek charges. The mountain freshness was animated with a mixture of the fetid odor of horse excrement, the woody smell of sawdust, pungent liniment and fragrant timothy hay. But this mood of excitement did nothing to quicken J.P.'s pulse. For him, it was routine. He had sent more mounts to parade in front of one grand-

24

stand or another than he cared to recall. Stoically he went about the task of getting Paragon ready for the race scheduled for eleven thirty.

It was a long, winding trail of horse tracks that led J.P. to the racing turf. Raised on a remote ranch in the Guadalupe Mountains, and too headstrong and wild for the young woman who taught in the one room school, he was packed off to the New Mexico Military Institute for his secondary education. His parents hoped that supervised, schooled and disciplined as a cadet in a military regime he might change. That, like a young bronco in the hands of a good bronc buster, he might be broken to lead and absorb some formal education at the same time.

J.P.'s experience and natural ability in handling horses saw him to a membership on the school's polo team. In his sophomore year his almost exclusive devotion to horses and the game of polo all but eliminated his attention to his studies. As a consequence of failing grades and demerits for insubordination he was drummed out of the institution. He played professional polo for two seasons. He found the challenge and excitement on the playing field, the ego-building conquests of socialite girls at the after-game parties, and good horses to ride fit with his idea of the good life.

Polo is a sport of the gentry. Talented with horses and mallet, but with manners more suited to the barn than to the parlor and with all his worldly possessions fitting into his footlocker which smelled of dirty socks and Absorbine Jr., J P. matured to the disillusionment that he was nothing more than a hired hand. Being a five goal player did nothing off the playing field toward elevating him above his caste as a lackey. Smarting from a put down from the daughter of the owner of a string of horses he was playing, J.P. quit the sport and moved to the one-on-one, rough-and-tumble world of professional rodeo. His temperament was better suited to contesting the abilities of bucking horses and brahma bulls where a man was measured by his guts and abilities, not his pedigree or finesse.

He spent the next eight years following the rodeo circuits, from the championship contests at the Cow Palace in San Francisco to pumpkin-rollers at the county fair grounds in Podunk. A trail of a million miles littered with cigarette butts and empty bottles, more wild women than he could recall and too many rank horses and fighting bulls had left J.P. with a crushed vertebra and a silver trophy buckle so scarred from the scratches of phosphorous-tipped matches that it had no value as a pawn.

More and more frequently in the latter part of those years there were those times when he would wake up sharing a bed in a cheap motel room with

25

a frowsy companion and a throbbing head that punished him with every beat of his heart. Staggering into a bathroom he would see an unkempt and bleary-eyed stranger staring back from the mirror. Into a fold of his whiskey-fogged brain would come the sobering realization that his need for a drink had gone far beyond the sociable party-time toddy. Now it was an undeniable subconscious craving for the ego-building stimulant that gave him the illusion of being buoyed from the quicksand of inferiority and self-condemnation.

It would be when his wallet was empty and his gut retched clean, when he was seized so badly by the tremors that it took two hands to hold a glass to his parched mouth, and his mind and body screamed at him for the relief of "just one little drink," that he would face the reality of being a damned drunk. These periods of penitence and flagellation and a determined decision to go on the wagon were spasmodic, and always bracketed by two or three day binges.

J.P. met Virginia when he was working as a stable hand mucking out stalls at Sunland Park race track near El Paso. She was one of those people who carry the cross of undeniable compassion and affection for the down-and-outers, the strays of life. She would pick up J.P.'s meal tab whenever she waited on him at the cafe and suspected he was down to his last few coins.

One of seven living children and three siblings that had died in infancy, Virginia grew to her teens as a member of the Jake Spence family of itinerant farm workers. Her father was a domineering drunk who could not keep his hands off of his daughters. It had not taken much sweet-talk and persuasion from Bob Smith, a swaggering, brilliantined jockey to entice Virginia to run away and join him as he followed the racehorses.

They were in El Paso for the winter racing season when he came staggering into their twenty-five dollar a week motel room. He was drunk and belligerent. They quarreled. He attacked her, first with his fists until she was on the floor, then with his belt, flaying her with the heavy buckle. She crawled under the bed to get away from him. He gathered his extra shirt and Wranglers, her money out of her purse and slammed the door behind him.

Mae, the motel manager, gave Virginia credit on her room rent while black eyes and facial bruises were healing. Virginia survived those ten days on the few meals her pride would let her accept from Mae and a few dollars she earned cleaning rooms. When she was presentable, she went back to her job waiting tables in the cafe.

J.P. would pass the time of day with Virginia over coffee, and he would not argue too hard when she offered to pick up his tab. Pride went before the fall for J.P. A score of women had come and gone through his life. When he was a top hand in Rodeo Cowboy's Association and had a choice, his preference ran to those with good looks, money or both. When he finally got around to taking notice of Virginia he saw a young woman with self-styled brown hair, pale blue eyes that were too big for her hungry, freckled face, and a boyish figure under a cheap, cotton dress. She was cut from a different bolt of cloth than were the good-lookers in their tight-fitting western clothes that he saw around the backside.

It took most of the winter racing season for J.P. to come to the realization that beauty was skin-deep, and the homely waitress behind the counter had a predominant inner beauty. Maybe it was the compassion, the tenderness in her eyes and her restraint from passing judgment when he was wallowing in the gutter of remorse and suffering from a hangover that illuminated a loving, kind soul and drew him to her.

Their friendship time over coffee, a kind word, and a reciprocal need took wing. They found themselves gravitating toward each other, then clinging in their mutual longing for companionship and love. They bolstered their individual weaknesses and shared their strengths to battle against the battering, demeaning winds of their lives.

Leaning on Virginia, and encouraged by her, J.P. did not touch anything stronger than coffee for three months. He saved enough to buy a western suit at a thrift shop and a gold wedding band out of a pawn shop. A justice of the peace married them and Mae gave them a crepe paper, Kool Aid, coffee and cupcake reception in the motel lobby.

Virginia's innate goodness and compassion, her unbounded capacity for loving, her blossoming beauty, and her insatiable hunger for love were J.P.'s salvation. She was his crutch that enabled him to walk like a man again. She took him by the hand and with unremitting patience as a mordant for her love, she cajoled a willing, but sometimes weak, J.P. down the rocky road to sobriety. She gave him reason to rekindle his almost-dead ambition. More to make her proud, and carried by her unwavering faith, he picked himself up by his boot pulls. He worked his way from an unreliable stable hand to a widely-known and sought-after trainer of racehorses.

Life for J.P. consisted of three things: sending good horses across the finish line ahead of the field, his wife Virginia and their daughter Lynn.

At forty-five, when J.P. went to work for Dock, he looked like he might be crowding fifty-five. It was not so much the years that marked his features as it was the miles and rough country over which he had travelled those miles.

A stranger, sizing J.P. up, would never figure him for a shoe clerk. A gray Resistol was pulled low over faded blue eyes which were partially concealed by a perpetual scowl against cigarette smoke, the elements of life and the weather. His black, thinning hair flecked with gray over a clean-shaven angular face aged by sun and wind, thick wrists and scarred hands, bowlegged and flat-assed saddlemen's jeans belted low around slim hips, and scuffed boots all marked him as being bent as a sapling that grew to maturity on the hardscrabble side of the equestrian industry. A heavily veined nose and nicotine-stained fingers spoke of recurring bouts with alcohol and tobacco addictions. J.P. was a hard-twisted, lean man who could stand flat footed and be at eye level with the withers of a horse measuring fifteen hands.

Walking along behind as Tommy the stable boy led Paragon from the barns toward the paddock, J.P. studied the horse's movements, looking for any sign of lameness or weakness. But his thoughts were not wholly committed to the task. He knew the horse was sound. Paragon was ready. From here to the finish line it was up to the breaks and Sonny.

A frown contorted his features as he flipped his cigarette butt onto the manicured lawn bordering the pathway. "I ought to be feelin' on top of the world," he muttered to himself. "I haven't had a drink in over ten months, and this is the first decent horse I've had to work with since they suspended me at Los Alamitos five years ago.

"Five goddamn long, lean, wasted years," he grumbled as his thoughts turned to reminiscing. It seemed to him, in retrospect, that he had lived in a vacuum for an eternity since his suspension. It was hard to clearly recall the days when he had been on top. Back when he could pick the stable he wanted to train for and name his own price. He and Virginia had lived high on the hog in those days. Virginia wore nice clothes and went to a shop to have her hair and nails done by a beautician. They drove a new car each year and lived in nice homes. "Hell," J.P. grunted, "I thought nothing of paying four hundred dollars for a pair of boots or two hundred for a hat."

I got greedy, wanted even more, he thought. I knew damned well that filly didn't have enough heart to win her race; she'd never shown any stayin' power. She had the leg and the reach if a man could just get her to put out for the distance. The handicappers sure had her pegged. She went on the board payin' seventy-three, and at the close of betting the board still showed her carryin' odds of sixty-five. Shit, I was ashamed to have my name tacked on the bitch as her trainer. And I damned sure wouldn't have had if the old man hadn't made me agree to take her in as part of the package deal.

28

J.P. slowly shook his head and pursed his lips in reflection as he recalled that day six years ago when Maiden's Prayer had run in the third race at Los Alamitos. Those odds were just too damned tempting, he thought. I couldn't resist a chance at some easy money. A slug of "elephant juice," camouflaged by some "bute" should have put a fire under her tail. It should've charged the dead-headed bitch to where she would go the distance without coastin'. Hyped up, there was a better than even chance that she would run in the money.

J.P.'s scowl deepened as the disturbing memory flooded his mind. Damnit to hell, he groused to himself, I had to tell Leroy that the filly was loaded and how I wanted her ridden. Of course, the little shit went and laid a big bet on her. Then the dumb bastard, instead of easing her along like I told him, had to get excited and go to the bat right out of the gate. If he'd a just let her warm up slowly, like I told him, things would have been different. But he pushed her too hard. Instead of the drug being absorbed slowly, the whole dose hit her heart all at once.

I'll never, as long as I live, be able to get that picture out of my mind, he reflected. There she was, ahead by half a length coming into the stretch, runnin' like she'd never run in her life, when she staggered a couple of steps. Then she dropped like she'd been pole-axed. The examining vet said the valves in her heart ruptured from the large dose of stimulation.

"Stupid little shit," J.P. exclaimed at the vivid memory of Maiden's Prayer falling in mid-stride, spilling the jockey beneath the feet of running horses, and the piercing screams from the spectators in the grandstand.

"You talkin' to me?" Tommy turned to look back at J.P.

"No," J.P. grunted. "Go on. It's all right. I was talkin' to myself."

As they turned into the paddock area, J.P. looked around at the other trainers readying their horses for the upcoming race. I sure as hell wasn't the first man to hype a horse, and damned sure won't be the last, he thought. The goddamn commissioners were too hard on me.

Tommy led Paragon into their assigned stall. J.P. took the halter shank from him and watched as Tommy and Sonny set Sonny's saddle. But his mind would not turn loose of the Los Alamitos race. The filly going down right in front of the grandstand, and them gapin', screamin' idiots didn't help my case none. I know damned well I have no one to blame but myself, and I knew it then, but I just couldn't take it. Losing my license. All the bad-mouthin' by a bunch of back-stabbin' bastards I thought were my friends. They couldn't wait to get a kick in at me when I was down.

Virginia took it better than I did, J.P. reflected. I've got to give her credit.

She sure as hell tried to help me over the rough spots. It was me goin' back to the bottle that finally got her down. She hated that worse than me losing my license, or the fact that she had to go back to waitin' tables so we could eat. She stuck it out for four years before she tore up her ticket. I know now that I was a piss-poor husband, and I don't know how she put up with me as long as she did. She used to say I was just feeling sorry for myself, that I didn't give a damn about how it was for her and Lynn, and by God, she was right. I was only thinkin' about myself.

J.P. shook his head over the memory. I went straight to hell in a handcart after she took Lynn and left me, he brooded. If it hadn't been for ole Ross Malone remembering me and what I could do with a green horse, hadn't recommended me to Dock, and him willing to give me a chance, I'd probably be down on First Street with the winos, or in a box in some Potter's field pushin' up weeds.

The time-worn, not-to-be-denied penance having run it's course, J.P.'s thoughts moved to the activities at hand. He stepped over to give Sonny a leg up to mount. "Ride to win," he instructed the jockey.

5

"Remember Vince, you sent me and Louie down to the barns to look at that black horse after he won the Texas race. I told you then he looked like he could run. You saw it, he damned near beat that gray filly. A little further an' I think he would've."

"What do you think, Marvin? You're the horse trainer."

"I've been watching Paragon, Mister Scavarda," Marvin Yeager replied. "I had my glasses on him when he came out of the gate. He broke slow. It looked to me like he might've forged the first step out of the box."

"What do you mean, by 'forged'?" Scavarda asked.

"A hind foot comes forward a little too far and strikes the front foot," Yeager answered. "That breaks the rhythm and the front foot doesn't quite get the reach it should. Being off balance causes a horse to lose a split second. In a short race, split seconds matter. I think that's what happened to Paragon. That split second advantage gave Gray Badger the lead. Paragon tried like hell but just couldn't overtake her in a three hundred and thirty yard run. I agree with Manny. If it'd been a two furlong race, I believe Paragon would've pushed ahead."

The three men watched from a private box in the Jockey Club as the ten horses were brought back along the track in front of the grandstand, headed for the paddock to be unsaddled. Scavarda, seated in the middle of the trio, lit a cigar and watched the procession through a cloud of gray smoke from the imported Havana. He extinguished the match with an exhalation and flipped it over the railing into the seat in front of him. He turned to the man at his left. "Marvin, you said after the Texas race that I oughta buy that black horse. What do you say now that he lost a race?"

"I still think you should consider it," Yeager replied.

The older man made no reply. Pensively he rotated the cigar between thumb and forefinger as he held it in his pursed lips. Rays of the midday sun shafting through a skylight reflected in dazzling flashes off the facets of a diamond ring on his moving hand. Scavarda turned in his seat to face Yeager. Thick, horn rimmed glasses accentuated heavy eyebrows and cold, calculating eyes. "I got a goddamn barn full of shittin' horses. Why in the hell do I need another one?" he asked.

"Paragon posted a record time in the Texas Futurity, his first major race," the trainer replied, "and I'm sure that his time will qualify him for the Oklahoma. I know that his breeding's not what's popular right now, but I'm acquainted with his sire and dam. The lineage may not be what you're reading about today, but this horse is bred to run. You told me you went to the backside to look at him yourself. What did you think?"

Scavarda placed his feet, clad in alligator black loafers, against the pipe railing which fronted the box. He reared back in his seat. Engrossed in thought, he toyed with his cigar like a child would savor a sucker. His blue suede sports coat had the collar of a white silk shirt folded over the coat collar. The shirt was open around a short, thick-set neck, exposing a hairy chest. Natty, gray serge trousers and black silk socks completed his tailored, coordinated attire. A fixed scowl and the shadow of a heavy beard darkened his fleshy features. He took the cigar from his mouth with deliberation and used a manicured nail on his little finger to flick the long ash of the cigar onto the floor. "Yeah," he said as he studied the cigar, "Manny an' me went to look at the horse. He's black and looks to be sound. That's all I could see. I may own a stable full of hay-eatin' nags, but I don't claim to be no shit-kickin' horseman. That's why you're on the payroll, Marvin."

"Well, Mister Scavarda, "Marvin said," you saw him run today and you...."

Scavarda jerked the cigar from his mouth and growled: "Wait a minute, Marvin. Yeah, I saw the son-of-a-bitch run today. And you say he ran a good race in Texas last week. But how in the hell do I know he wasn't juiced up? You told me his trainer had been booted off the track for dopin' a horse. And you told me he's a boozer. Shit, I don't trust a man with that kind of reputation. He's probably mainlining the fuckin' horse. Got the son-of-a-bitch hooked on an expensive habit; like some of my high-society, patsy friends are." He stuck the cigar back in his mouth. A smug smile over his clever comparison began to work at the corners of his mouth. "I'd buy the cocksucker an' he'd probably drop dead from withdrawals before you'd get him to my barn."

"I don't think he's runnin' on dope, Mister Scavarda," the hired horseman ventured. "I looked him over good after the futurity. He didn't act like a horse that was hopped up, and the urine test showed he was clean. Anyway, it's no

32

a practice to hype a horse runnin' in a main event because the vets run a lot of tests on the winners, or any horse that acts like it's been tampered with.

"I've done some talkin' on the backside. Seems like Bates, Paragon's trainer, is on the wagon and playing the game straight now. The word is that this Paragon can cut it without a boost," he added.

"You still haven't told me why I need the damned horse," Scavarda said as he turned his attention to the racing program to check out the upcoming race. "We got a barn full of runnin' horses and it's costin' me a bundle to feed 'em an' pay all you shit-kickers to baby 'em. Huh!" he snorted. "My ole man would have a shittin' hemorrhage if he knew how much money I spend on horses. He rode one to the mine every day an' I'll bet he never spent a dime on that ole nag."

"Mister Scavarda," the horse trainer said, "even though this horse has won a futurity, he's still an unknown. Few people know anything about his breeding. Most people never heard of his sire or his dam. Trainham, who owns him, is a rancher from West Texas who just lucked onto the horse. He's not into the racing industry. Paragon's the only horse he's got running, and it's his first season.

"What you might consider," Marvin went on, "is this: if the horse has it in him, like I think he does, he'll sure be a strong contender in the Oklahoma Futurity and he'll have a good chance of qualifying for the Rainbow. Like I said, Mister Scavarda, these futurities are policed pretty close. Only the top contenders are competing, so nobody takes any chances hyping their horses. They run a clean race. That's why a natural, like this Paragon, one that can run a hole in the wind without any chemicals, might prove to be a dark horse in the futurities. It's only happened here twice before, but I've got a hunch that we might see that black stud capture the Triple Crown. It's a long shot, I know, but I think the horse has the ability. Bates is a top trainer and their jockey is one of the best."

Scavarda's brow knitted and his eyes narrowed as he studied the trainer's comments. He turned his attention to the tote board posting the horses and their odds for the next race. "Manny, go put me down for two cees on the nose of the four horse," he ordered. "An' hey," he called after the departing man, "bring me a Royale and Seven." He turned his attention back to Marvin. "So you think this Paragon horse's got the goods?"

"Yes sir I do, that's one of two reasons why you might want to try and buy...."

Scavarda interrupted to snap: "Yeager, I don't try to buy anything. If I want to buy something, shit, I buy it. Understand? There're ways to handle these cocksuckers who try to bait me, or think they can hold me up. They learn pretty quick that they're not dealin' with a dumb-ass. I figure everything and everybody's got a price and if they're gonna deal with me, they deal on my terms, or we don't deal. Remember that, Yeager."

"Well," Marvin said slowly, rolling with the censure, "I think the value of the horse lies not only in his running ability but in his breeding. Paragon is one of a kind. His bloodline can't be duplicated. He won the Texas and qualified today for the Oklahoma. Win or lose that one, I think Trainham will nominate him for the Rainbow. If the horse were to win the Oklahoma, there's the possibility he just might win the Triple Crown. If he shows the heart and the speed to win, I think breeders will be wanting to incorporate his bloodline with theirs. You could set him up at your breeding farm and name your price for his services. The stud's a coming three and his future is all ahead of him. You'd have his track purses, plus breeding fees. If his ability to run carries over to his get, you'd have a foundation sire."

"What kind of money we talkin' about?" Scavarda asked.

"I don't know," Yeager replied. "I do know that Trainham bought Paragon's dam at an auction for the price of a killer. She was carrying the service of Wall Street so the colt was a bonus. As I said, this is his first venture into racing. He might be glad to gather up his marbles and call it quits while he's ahead. Maybe he'd be happy to pocket another hundred grand and go back to the ranch."

The older man sat silently, slowly rolling the cigar in his pursed lips. Marvin concentrated on the current Racing Form, as if the subject was dead. Scavarda dropped the partially smoked Havana on the concrete floor, ground the fire out with his shoe and snapped: "Okay. Go buy the damned nag. Offer the cowboy eighty grand. What the hell," he said in an almost jocular tone of voice, "if he don't win big here like you think he will, you can haul him to Jersey an' I'll sell him to one of those horse-lovin' dumb-butts back there for a hundred and twenty."

6

Dock tried to bring his thoughts to bear on the evening paper. J.P. chain-smoked while he paced the floor. They were waiting on a call from the track that would report whether or not Paragon's time in the morning race qualified him for the Oklahoma Futurity. J.P. stopped in front of the picture window to look out on Sierra Vista and the mountain in the background. He said over his shoulder: "Dock, if we make it, and run a good race in the Futurity, I'm going to ask you for a favor."

Dock lowered his paper and replied: "What can I do for you?"

"Well, I'm hopin' to get up enough nerve to call Virginia and ask her if she'll come back to me. If she's agreeable, I'll want to move her here, but I'll need a pickup to haul her stuff. I couldn't get it all in my car, and I'm not sure that old clunker of mine would make the trip. I'd like to borrow your pickup."

"You'll be more than welcome to it, J.P. From what little you've told me about your wife and daughter, I think it would be the best medicine in the world for you if you all could get back together again."

"Well," J.P. said as he turned to face Dock, "working with you and Paragon has given me a new lease on life. Because of you two, I'm stayin' busy an' got lots on my mind. My ole man used to say that an idle mind was the devil's workshop. Funny thing, I remember thinkin' when I was a young fellow that my dad didn't have enough smarts to pour piss out of a boot. Guess it was because he was just a hard workin' old cowpuncher. Now I can see some sense in the things he used to preach to me."

"Sometimes," Dock responded, "I think we dads preach too much. Kids classify it all as bull shit and it turns them off."

"Anyway," J.P. went on, "my life's taken a turn for the better, but without Virginia and Lynn to share it with me, it doesn't have the zest it ought to. I miss havin' Virginia waitin' for me in the evening, ready to share the day's experiences. Dock, she may not be Miss America, but I'm here to tell you, she's beautiful to me. Kinda like a horse I rode one time. It wouldn't take a blue ribbon at the county fair but the old bugger had a heart as big as all outdoors an' you could count on him as sure as the sun'll rise tomorrow.

"I miss my daughter too," J.P. continued, as he walked over to sit on the edge of the bed. "I miss her walkin' alongside me, tellin' me about some new trick she'd figured out in handlin' a green colt."

Dock sat and listened. He saw the tears well in the eyes of the tough trainer. He thought of his Martha, and a catch caught in his throat. J.P. rose and went back to the window to stand with his back toward Dock as he self-consciously wiped the tears on his shirt sleeve. "That girl's gonna be a horsewoman, Dock," he said after a moment. "You say I have a way with horses, but I'm the first to admit that Lynn can take a colt that'd give me trouble and she can sweet-talk it into following her around like a puppy dog. Of course, I've had her with me around horses since she was just a little shaver. Virginia used to worry about her gettin' hurt, but you know, it seems like most horses have a special feeling for little kids. Why, I've seen horses that would eat a man's lunch, but were gentle as a kitten with a kid on 'em."

"That's true, J.P. Some kids seem to have a natural affinity, a feeling for animals. The animals can sense it too, and they respond." Dock said as he folded up the newspaper and rose from the chair. "But that's not always true. Some kids have the opposite affect. They're either mean to an animal or afraid of it, and animals sense that and react to it. I'm sorry to say that my stepson Patrick falls in the latter group. He's been around pets and stock most of his life, but he's never developed a feeling for them." Dock walked over to stand beside J.P. and look out the window. "Martha and I figured he'd take over the ranch someday, but I don't know. He's a poor hand horseback. He's so damned afraid of one with some spirit that he won't hardly get it out of a walk. But then he's hell on a gentle one. He's always whippin', spurrin', and jerkin' it around. He doesn't have the patience it takes to handle animals. I just don't know," Dock puzzled, shaking his head.

"You've never said much about your stepson," J.P. said.

"Well," Dock said as he thrust his hands into the pockets of his pants. "Patrick is Martha's boy by her first husband. He was just a baby when Martha and I married. I adopted him when he was a yearling."

"Is he all the family you have?" J.P. inquired.

"Yep," Dock replied. He turned away from the window, walked over to gather his hat from the bureau and said, "Let's go eat. I'm hungry. I'll leave word at the front desk to forward my calls to the dining room."

J.P. watched as Dock made his way back through the crowded restaurant toward their table. He pulled out a chair and sat down. Neither man spoke as Dock meticulously spread his napkin in his lap. His features were expressionless, like that of a good poker player in a high-stakes game of stud. He hates to break the bad news to me, J.P. thought. A wave of disappointment passed over him as the thought of what might've been vaporized. He dropped his questioning eyes from Dock's face and resumed eating, without an appetite.

Dock cleared his throat. When J.P. looked at him, Dock said with a forced effort of nonchalance, "That was the call we've been waitin' for." He cleared his throat again. A little smile worked at the corners of his mouth. "J.P., our horse has qualified for the Oklahoma Futurity." Two faces, worn and creased by time, worries and weather softened as the veil of anxiety faded into matching smiles of achievement.

They had ten days to wait. Ten days to maintain their horse in the ready. Ten days to study the other nine contenders. Ten days for J.P. to assess it all and plan strategy. Ten days for nerves to fray under the building stress of suspense.

"Come in," Dock said as he opened the motel room door. "Come in and sit down. I'll just be a minute. I'm on the phone, checking on how things are at the ranch." J.P. took a seat as Dock went back to the telephone. "Mario," he said into the receiver, *"dígame."* Dock's face was a study in concentration as he listened to the lengthy reply. He looked over at J.P. and opened his eyes wide as a smile crossed his face. *"Dos pulgados, y se cayó muy despacio?"* He continued after a pause, *"Qué bueno, Mario. Váyase con cuidado. Adios."* Dock replaced the receiver. He turned to J.P. and said, "We had a two inch rain at the ranch an' it was a good slow one, not one of those damned gully-washers like we usually get this time of year."

"That ought to make you sleep better," J.P. commented. "Won't that put some life back in your pasture grass before the frosts?"

"Yeah," Dock replied. "And it'll soften up the old grass and grow some winter weeds."

"You got a Mexican stayin' at the ranch?" J.P. asked.

"Yeah, a wet-back from La Paz, a little village down near Chihuahua. He's been with me for about eight years. Goes home to plant his crops or harvest, and I don't think he's missed a year gettin' his wife pregnant. Then he comes back to the ranch, broke, but smiling. He's a helluva good man. Only problem is, he's reluctant as hell to speak what little English he knows. He won't hardly use the phone, says he can't make the operator understand what he wants. So I have to try to catch him in the bunkhouse when I want to find out how things are going."

"Isn't your boy there at the ranch?" J.P. asked.

"He comes and goes," Dock mumbled after some hesitation. "Shows up mostly when he's hungry, broke, or both. I can't depend on him so I keep Mario there to look after things. You ready to go eat?" They were walking out the door when the phone rang. "Go get us a table, J.P., I'll see what this call is and be right along."

The motel dining room, decorated with southwestern paintings on the walls, chandeliers fashioned out of simulated Conestoga wagon wheels and rustic, ranch-style furniture, was crowded with weekend tourists. The general atmosphere was one of gaiety and affluence. The droning of voices was punctuated frequently by outbursts of polite laughter from the customers. Their accents and dress made it obvious that the majority of the diners hailed from the Southwest. They were people flush with expendable funds set aside for vacationing. Money that was spawned by the drilling rigs and pump jacks that probed beneath the surfaces of Oklahoma and Texas for oil and gas, money derived from the vast herds of cattle and sheep that grazed the pasturelands and from the fertile fields where the turning plows had replaced the buffalo sod with golden waves of grain. Dock saw J.P. in one of the booths along the far wall. He slid into the seat across from the trainer. "Have you ordered?" he asked.

"No, I was waitin' for you," J.P. replied.

After the waitress had taken their orders, Dock leaned across the table and asked quietly: "Do you know a man named Marvin Yeager?"

"Yeah," J.P. answered. "He's a trainer. Works for a stable out of New Jersey owned by a man named Vince Scavarda. They're runnin' some horses here this summer. Rumor has it that there's mob money backing the whole deal."

"Well, that was this Yeager fellow on the phone," Dock said. "Asked if we could get together over breakfast tomorrow. He didn't say what was on his mind. Just said that he'd like to meet me here at six o'clock tomorrow morning."

J.P. studied his coffee cup for a long moment, then suggested: "Maybe he's huntin' a job." The waitress brought their salad dishes and the two men dispensed with conversation while they ate.

"The Scavarda stable used to handle mostly thoroughbreds," J.P. commented, as he pushed his salad plate aside. "But I see where they've been picking up some decent quarter horses. I don't know much about Yeager. I've met him a few times. We talked horses mostly. He's kind of a quiet fellow. Seems to stay pretty much near his own barn. He appears to be a decent sort of guy from what little I know of him. The word around the backside is that he's a good hand with a horse, but that Scavarda doesn't know shit from Shinola about horseflesh, and he's heavy-handed when it comes to dealin' with people. They say he keeps a tight rein on Yeager. So, maybe Yeager's tired of it and's decided to look for a greener pasture."

"Well, I can't imagine what he wants with me. He surely knows that you're training for me," Dock puzzled aloud.

7

The tall, dark-complexioned man walked through the restaurant to stand beside Dock's table. "Good morning," he said.

"Good mornin'," Dock replied as he took in the standard horseman's attire of blue denim Levi trousers, a white, long-sleeved dress shirt, and western hat.

"I'm Marvin Yeager," the man said as he stuck his hand out over the table.

Dock took the man's hand and responded with a firm handshake. "I figure you know I'm Dock Trainham. Have a seat." Dock evaluated the man as Yeager walked back across the room to hang his hat on the clothes tree beside the cashier's station and returned to the table. One side or the other of forty, Dock figured. Scuffed boots with spur marks on the heel counters and the man's lean frame told him that Yeager was a hands-on, working horseman. As Yeager pulled out a chair and sat down at the table, Dock asked: "Had breakfast yet?"

"No sir," Yeager replied.

"Good. Hand me that cup there and I'll pour you some of this starting fluid." He filled the cup from the carafe and looked at the man as he handed the cup to him. He took in the straight, black hair, high cheekbones and dark eyes. He's got Indian blood in his veins, Dock thought, and he just might be a natural with horses. The two men eased into their meeting by sipping their coffee in silence. The waitress came and took Yeager's order for two eggs over-easy, hash browns, toast and bacon. Dock ordered two scrambled eggs with salsa verde, biscuits and bacon. Over their second cup of coffee they made small talk about the weather and such. After breakfast they worked closer to the bone and talked horses and racing. Yeager volunteered that he was from Fairfax, Oklahoma and Dock mentioned that he had been there. He had bought a load of bulls from an Osage, Hereford breeder. Yeager allowed that his grandmother had been a full-blooded Osage Indian. He told the Texas rancher that he'd started out on the track as a groom and then an exercise boy at a county track near Bartlesville.

Yeager pulled a pack of cigarettes from his shirt pocket and offered it to Dock. "No thanks," Dock replied, "gave them up a couple of years ago." Yeager returned the pack to his pocket without shaking one out for himself. "I've tried to quit," he said, "so I won't tempt you by blowing smoke in your face."

"It won't bother me if you light up," Dock offered. "I remember how good they tasted after breakfast. Guess that's the one I miss the most."

"Mister Trainham," Yeager said, "your black stud has caught the attention of my boss. He sent me to ask if you'd consider selling him."

Dock looked at Yeager for a long moment, then let his gaze wander absently around at the people coming into the restaurant as he digested the query. He toyed with his coffee cup as he turned the proposal over in his mind; considering parting with the horse, and the possible implications of the unexpected offer. The idea that Paragon had caught someone's eye was not surprising, when he stopped to think about it. The thought of parting with the stud colt was something he had not considered; not since Ross Malone had offered to buy him as a yearling. The money was certainly something to take into account. Money that could be applied to his bank note, relieving the pressure from the mortgage against the ranch. If I had that millstone from around my neck I could sure breath a lot easier, Dock thought. Realizing that his prolonged silence had become awkward, he spoke up: "I guess I'll have to admit that your offer comes as a surprise and catches me unprepared. To be truthful, Mister Yeager, I just haven't given any thought to selling the horse. I'm not even sure how I'd price him."

The congenial sounds of the breakfast crowd starting their day mingled with the clinking of dishes and eating utensils as waitresses and bus boys served the room full of diners. Yeager leaned into the table. He said, in a voice not intended to carry beyond Dock's ears, "Mister Scavarda is willing to pay you eighty thousand. He told me to tell you he'd pay it any way you wanted: all in cash, a check for partial payment and the remainder in cash, part up front and the rest, with interest, however and whenever you want it."

Dock fiddled with the salt shaker as he listened to the details of the proposition, his mind weighing the options. He could sell Paragon, take the money and go back to the ranch. Eighty thousand, or what would be left after taxes, should get the banker off his back. And he'd be back where he belonged. Back where he could look after his business instead of being here worrying about the condition of the cattle, the shape of the pastures and whether the windmills were all pumping. He'd be at home, not camping in a motel, eating in restaurants, and standing around with his hands in his pockets. He could take the money and let Scavarda worry about Paragon. Let him worry about the horse breaking a leg in a race or in the gate, going off his feed, or one of the many things that always seemed to be happening to these pampered race horses. Then on the other hand, Dock thought, there would be the parting with Paragon of Merit. Martha's horse. Another tie to Martha gone. And what about J.P. and his plans to put his family back together in the future? Could he stay away from the bottle, be able to get another horse to train, or would the disappointment be his undoing? Was Paragon his crutch for healing? And I'd always be wondering what might've been.

Dock's dilemma was obvious by his silent concentration and furrowed brow. Yeager leaned back toward him and said: "The trade would be completed when you sign the bill of sale and decide how you want to be paid. If you want delayed payment, Mister Scavarda will sign a note. To sweeten the deal he'll agree to you running Paragon in the Oklahoma under your silks. Any winnings would be split fifty-fifty. We wouldn't take full possession until after the race."

The pros and cons tugged at Dock's reasoning. Thoughts swirled and clouded his mind like dust devils in a March storm. He wished he were horseback, alone in one of the pastures back at the ranch instead of being in this noisy restaurant. He had always found he could take a problem apart and see each component better astride a good horse moving at an easy gait across wide open spaces. But that was not to be. Finally he looked at the man sitting patiently across from him and said: "Mister Yeager, you boys have given me a tough problem. One that I can't resolve here and now. Ask Mister Scavarda if he'll give me until tomorrow at noon to think on it."

"Here is his home phone," Yeager said as he stood and handed Dock a business card.

8

"Dock, we ought to go to the window and put some money down this afternoon," J.P. suggested.

"You got a hot tip straight from the horse's mouth?" Dock bantered as he looked up from his plate of bacon and eggs.

"Today's the day to bet on the long shots," J.P. replied.

"You mean the long shots run better on Thursdays? You pullin' an old country boy's leg, J.P.?"

"Why Dock, you know I wouldn't pull your leg," J.P. replied with a chuckle. "I'll tell you why it's a good day for wagerin' on the long shots, but wait until we're out in the pickup. I hate to disillusion these people," he said as he glanced around the dining room.

They waited in line to pay the cashier for their meals, made their way through the lobby crowded with milling vacationers and horse people, and walked out of the motel into an invigorating morning. An infinite sky, flawless as a blue diamond except for a single contrail which stretched across the heavens like a wispy strand of handspun wool, canopied the valley. The mountain air was washed clean by a heavy dew and perfumed with the fragrance of sun-warmed pine trees.

"You know," Dock said to J.P. as they drove east along the main thoroughfare headed for the track, "I'd a helluva lot rather bet on a likely-looking long shot than follow along with the housewives betting on the favorite to show. So, what makes today any different? Is there going to be a dark horse that pulls an upset?"

"Sonny slipped me the word," J.P. replied. "Today's the day the jockeys will try to put some feathers in their nests. There's likely to be a dark horse in a certain race that'll be carrying long odds. Chances are it'll run in the money."

"How does that figure?" Dock asked. "Do the jockeys know something about the horses that the handicappers don't?"

"Well, they might," J.P. said. "First off, they know that there'll be a horse in a certain race that's got the ability but for some reason goes on the board with long odds. Or, maybe the jockeys will get wind of a 'dog' that'll be hyped. Anyway, the boys riding in that race will try to handle their mounts so the long shot will run in the money."

"We talked about that, about a jockey holding his horse back," Dock said. "How can they get away with it without someone cryin' foul to the stewards?"

"Well, it doesn't always work because the boys have to be careful, of course. It can't be too obvious," J.P. replied. "Dock, you've seen that black fellow they call Simon who's kind of a shade-tree chiropractor and a rubdown man in the jockey's locker room, haven't you?"

"Yeah, I've seen him, but how does he figure in all this?"

"Well, he's the key. I'll hang around the big-dollar pari-mutuel window. When the time's right, Simon will come hustlin' up just before the window closes. He'll be carryin' a bundle of bettin' money gathered up from the jockeys. I'll just ease right in behind him, listen to how he lays the bets, and follow suit."

"I'll be dammed!" Dock exclaimed. "There's more damned finagling in this horse racin' business than there is in Washington politics. The poor sucker who puts his money down is bucking not only the horses' runnin' abilities and the pari-mutuel's odds but the whole darn system. Hell's fire, he looks at the horses, studies the tout sheets, weighs the horses' past performances, their speed indexes, checks their breeding, considers the abilities of the jockeys and the trainers. He weighs the handicaps, considers the track conditions, puts a wet finger up to check the wind, stops to consider if a certain horse's name might tie into a lucky omen, rubs his lucky charm and gives a little prayer. Then, the sucker places a bet on his choice, thinkin' he's got all the angles and the odds figured out.

"Now, J.P., I'm learning' from you that all that may not have a damned thing to do with which horses run in the money. The average bettor probably thinks the outcome of a race is a result of matching the horses' abilities. Hell's bells, he's bettin' against a stacked deck. Against what one horse can do competing with the field, the odds set by the handicappers, doped horses, bribed gate handlers and jockeys who don't ride to win. The whole shitaree's stacked against the poor boob," Dock exclaimed, shaking his head in disgust.

"Now Dock," J.P. remonstrated, "It's not all that bad. Sure, that stuff goes on, but it's the exception, not the rule. That's why we have stewards and commissioners. It's just like anything else where there's money at stake; it's

44

every man for himself, players beware, and suckers are the lifeblood and fair game.

"I've been around the tracks for a helluva long time. I've met a lot of good people; people who care about their horses. People who'd sure stoop to pick up a buck if it's lying around unattended but the same people who'd return your lost wallet with every dollar in it. Shit yes there're some bad apples. There're those who'll abuse their horses, have no feelin' for 'em. They're the ones who really chap my ass. An' there're those who aren't above cheatin' any way possible to line their pockets, without any pangs of conscience. The only time they might show remorse is if they get caught with their hand in the cookie jar. Then there's dammed few who'll admit any guilt. Most go to crawfishin'.

"I know what you're thinkin', Dock. Yeah, I broke the rules once. Bad. I was as sorry as the sorriest. Guilty as hell of trying to make a fast buck and not worried in the least what it might cost someone else. But thank God I got caught, and they hung me out to dry. I paid through the nose for my mistake, but I figure that lesson made me a better man in the long run. The smart-ass, greedy boys are runnin' against long odds on a sloppy track, and most generally they don't get away with their shenanigans too long. They get tripped up eventually, and their chickens come home to roost."

"You wanted to break the rules when you suggested that we have Sonny run Paragon to place instead of to win," Dock reminded J.P.

"Dock, you've got to understand, an' I'm not crawfishin', but pacing your horse, working into a position to create an advantage, then taking that advantage; working to better your odds and figuring your opponent's weaknesses are all part of the game. A trainer's like a coach, he plays those advantages. Look at it this way: You wouldn't think of force-feeding your cattle salt then turning them on water the night before you'd weigh them to a buyer, but you'd sure try to manage the delivery to where you'd get the best weigh-up possible, wouldn't you?"

Dock wheeled into the left turn lane, stopped to let an approaching eighteen wheeler barrel past, then drove the pickup through the gate marked Horseman's Entrance. After some deep thought, he said: "Maybe so, J.P., it's just that I can't see where the lines are between the white, the gray, and the black."

Something's damned sure bothering him, J.P. thought as he watched Dock idly stirring coffee that surely must be cold by now. As if he had picked up on J.P.'s thoughts, Dock laid the spoon on the table, pushed the untasted coffee to one side, leaned his forearms on the table, and confided: "J.P., I've got a problem."

J.P. moved in closer to the table. "Anything I can help you with?" he asked.

"Maybe," Dock drawled and leaned back to look thoughtfully at his trainer and friend.

Scavarda's offer to buy Paragon had disrupted Dock's night. He had awakened from a troubled sleep to turn on the bedside lamp and see that it was twelve-twenty. The rest of the night had been spent tossing and turning, trying to find a comfortable position from which he might court slumber. But his mind was not geared for sleep. Considering selling Paragon had brought disquieting thoughts. Thoughts about Martha. Nostalgic thoughts about her deep affection for the black colt. In his mind's eye he could see her in her gentle way of handling the colt, see her bottle feeding it to help the old mare. He thought on those last sorrowful days, when her eyes, lusterless from drugs and pain, would show a little spark of life when the yearling would come up to the fence in front of the house and nicker at her. These were bittersweet memories, but memories that persisted over the fading reminiscences of happier times.

That he was even considering selling Paragon bothered him. Martha's pet that had made her pain-racked days a little more bearable. In his mind's eye, in the darkened motel room, Dock could see her in the wheel chair, wasted and frail, reaching up to stroke the colt's velvety nose, talking sweet nonsense and exchanging glances with Dock with eyes that spoke of love and pride of man and horse. With her horse gone down the road, sold to a stranger for no telling what kind of life ahead, the memories would be sullied. She'd be there, if only in Dock's mind, when he drove into the yard with an empty horse trailer. She'd know. She'd probably understand. "After all," she'd whisper from somewhere in her darkened room that Dock had left as it was, "eighty thousand dollars is a lot of money. You did what was best. Now don't you fret about it."

But what about J.P.? Dock had brooded as he turned and tossed in the rumpled bed. What about J.P.'s plans to reunite with his wife and daughter. Martha, even though she didn't know them, would sure want to see the family together again. Selling Paragon would no doubt, have an effect on their lives. "And after all," Dock spoke into the darkness, "it was J.P.'s handling and training that had made the horse."

46

Dock had switched on the bedside light to see that it was 2:43. He threw the sheet back and got up to go to the bathroom. "I'd give him a cut of the money. He's entitled to it," Dock said to the wall as he stood over the commode. But, he thought as he headed back to the bed, even with some money behind him, can he go on? Has he reached solid footing, or without Paragon will he lose his self-esteem and go back to drinking?

It had been a long night, blighted with indecision. It had left Dock feeling wrung out as he sat with J.P. for their midmorning coffee break. "I told you I was to have breakfast yesterday with that Yeager fellow," he said, and noted the tightening of the jaw muscles and the frown that crossed J.P.'s face, like the shadow of a moving storm cloud.

"Yeah, you mentioned it," J.P. responded in a constrained voice.

"Well, I couldn't figure what he'd want to talk to me about," Dock said, "and what he said puzzled me even more."

"Oh?" J.P. mumbled.

"He brought me an offer from his boss, Scavarda. They want to buy Paragon. What do you think of that?"

J.P. looked down into his coffee cup. Dock saw the knuckles that gripped the cup turn white. The cup trembled noticeably as J.P. slowly raised it to his mouth. His faded blue eyes hung on Dock over the rim of the cup and a clouded visage mirrored the unsettling thoughts that flooded his mind. "Well, that doesn't surprise me too much," J.P. replied as he lowered the cup to the table. "What do you aim to do?"

"I haven't made up my mind," Dock responded slowly.

"It's none of my business," J.P. said, "but can I ask you what kind of a deal they offered?"

"Eighty thousand," Dock answered in a low voice. "My terms would be thirty up front in escrow. They have agreed to let us run Paragon in the Oklahoma and pocket half of any winnings. After the race; win, lose, or draw they take full possession for the escrow money plus fifty thousand, cash. If anything beyond our control happens to the horse before closing, or Scavarda changes his mind, the thirty thousand is mine and the deal is off."

Both men sat in silence, oblivious to anything but their individual thoughts. J.P. fumbled with trembling fingers to work a cigarette out of the package in his shirt pocket. Dock toyed with a spoon on the table. A passing waitress who stopped to refill their coffee cups broke their concentration. "What do you think?" Dock asked.

"I don't know," J.P. replied in a barely audible voice. "As the horse stands today, I guess that's a fair price. If I had any way in hell of raisin' eighty grand, I'd damned sure pay it, if that's what you want for the horse. If the colt proves out like I think he will, he's worth a helluva lot more than that. But, who's to say. That's the gamble in the business of running horses."

"I know," Dock slowly nodded his head in agreement. He leaned on his forearms braced on the table, ignoring the fresh coffee.

J.P. hunched over the table, smoking and sipping on his coffee as his gaze moved restlessly around the dining room, but always going back to fasten on Dock. Finally he said over a deep sigh: "I guess I know what I'd do, but you've got to remember that I'm a dyed-in-the-wool racehorse man and gambling's part of my way of life. I'm not trying to influence you, Dock, but you asked me for my opinion, so I'm gonna give it to you.

"From my point of view, which might not be worth a plug nickel, I think your black stallion will make racing history. On the other hand, he could break a leg or turn sour tomorrow. Who knows?"

"I've thought of that," Dock said. "It's all a gamble, but I'm not a gamblin' man."

Both men lapsed into silence, immersed in their thoughts about what the sale of Paragon of Merit would mean to each of them. It was Dock, some minutes later, who broke the silence: "I say I'm not a gamblin' man, but hell, that's not true. I gamble for my livelihood every day of my life, trying to wrestle a living off my handful of cattle. I stake everything I can beg, borrow, or steal against the weather, disease and sickness in the herd, government edicts and USDA regulations, the fluctuations of the cattle market and where the Chicago Board of Trade pegs the future cattle and grain markets. Hell's fire, J.P., ranchin' for a living in West Texas makes the gamblers in Vegas look like pikers."

Dock sat back in his chair, his hands gripping the table edge, the cloud of uncertainty replaced by a set to his jaw and a glint in his eyes. "I am a gamblin' man, J.P., and I'm gonna gamble on Martha's Paragon of Merit. Will you go over and talk to Yeager? Tell him we appreciate his boss' interest in our horse and his offer, but the horse isn't for sale."

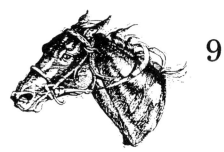

9

"Wayne! What the hell you doin' here?" J.P. exclaimed as he stepped into the living room of his rented bungalow to confront the dapperly-dressed man lounging in the recliner. "How'd you find me? An' how the hell did you get in? I know I locked the door when I left this morning."

The man slowly folded up the newspaper he had been reading and dropped it on the floor beside the chair. "Why, J.P., you're a man of notoriety since your horse won the Futurity. Finding where you live was just a matter of asking a few questions in the right places. As for the lock, you wouldn't want me to sit out there in a hot car waitin' for you to get home, would you? My plastic credit card can open more than charge accounts."

J.P. gave a derisive snort. "You're still the same old Wayne Belcheff," he said as he walked through the drab, disheveled living room into a kitchenette to set a brown paper grocery sack on a table.

"Where the hell you got your booze stashed, J.P.? I was gonna fix me a drink, but I couldn't even find a beer."

"I'm off the stuff, Wayne. I haven't had a drink in almost a year."

"The hell you say," Wayne said through a cloud of smoke from a freshly lit cigarette. "What put you on the wagon?"

"Well, I guess I finally realized that I just can't handle the stuff. It damned near ruined my life before I sobered up enough to see where I was headed. As my dad used to say, 'too soon we get old and too late we get smart.'"

"Most drunks take spells on the wagon," Wayne said. "The hard part is stayin' with it. How'd you handle that?"

J.P. took a small aluminum coffee pot from the dish drainer and started running tap water into it. "I'll fix us some coffee," he offered.

"You didn't answer me," Wayne prompted. "How you managing to stay away from the stuff? Livin' in this dump and hanging around with a bunch of track bums would damned sure drive me to drink."

"Well," J.P. replied rather reluctantly. "It's a long story. You remember Ross Malone? He used to make some book with you on the ponies. Maybe still does, I don't know. I do know he gets his money down on the ponies pretty regular, and he sure as hell doesn't leave much of it behind. You know he's got a good eye for a horse and a memory like a bear trap when it comes to track records. Well, anyway, Ross was fixin' to buy some cattle from a rancher named Dock Trainham over in Texas when he spots a likely- looking coming two year old horse colt that was bred to run. To make a long story short, Ross convinced Trainham the colt showed promise and should be put on the track. Ross remembered me, knew I was between horses, and recommended me as trainer. Part of the deal was that I promised Ross and the owner I'd walk the straight and narrow. They got my word that I'd go on the wagon, and if I couldn't stay off the stuff I'd roll my bed and move on, with no hassle. I guess I had enough sense left to realize that it was my chance, and probably my last one, to rejoin the living; maybe even get my wife and daughter back. Anyway, I've stayed so busy working with Mister Trainham's horse that I've been able to keep my nose clean."

"Well, J.P., I'm glad to see you've finally wised up. I handle my share of booze. Shit, it's part of my business, but I'm too damn smart to let it get the best of me. That's like these smart-asses snortin' coke. Stupid! Let me tell you, J.P., there ain't an easier mark in a card game than some of those boys who are gettin' their smarts out of a bottle or a bag of coke. It sure makes 'em think they're card sharks, but shit, they can't find their ass with both hands. Talk about fleecing the lambs..." Wayne reared back in the recliner to laugh at the thought.

"I guess you're still making a living hustlin' suckers," J.P. ventured as he reached into the cupboard for two mugs.

"Now, J. P., you're doin' me an injustice. By God, I might just have my lawyer sue for defamation of character," Wayne broke into laughter again. His laughter ended abruptly in a fit of racking coughs. When he regained his composure he continued. "I agree with ole W. C. Fields: 'Never give a sucker an even break.' Shit, J.P., I don't have to hustle marks, especially if I pick who I play with. I like to contest those boys who win a game or two of gin or a round of poker at their country club then come runnin' over to my place to show me how good they are. In a game of gin I can generally figure what they're holding after the fourth or fifth discard. Poker and blackjack's the same. It's all in remembering the cards, knowing how the cards are running and being able to read people."

"I guess you're right, Wayne," J.P. agreed as he took the steam-spewing pot off the stove. "I haven't done much card playing since I left the rodeo crowd. But I'm like you with your card playing. When it comes to laying my money down on a nag, I damned sure want to know that I've got the edge. You an' I don't chance our money for the sport of it. The coffee's ready. You take it black, don't you."

Wayne left the recliner and moved over to the kitchen table. The hand that held his cup, pale and soft looking, with manicured nails, was in contrast to those of J.P.'s that were freckled and roughened by hard work and the elements. The one feature in common was nicotine-stained fingers.

"You still in Midland?" J.P. asked.

"Yeah," Wayne replied.

"Still got your private club?"

"Yeah."

"You were just getting started good when I was playing polo there," J.P. said. "That was about sixty-six, I think."

"Yeah, that's right," Wayne agreed. "That was when you an' the polo crowd belonged to the club. Those blue bloods were good customers."

The two men sat sipping slowly on the hot coffee, their thoughts turned back over twenty years.

It was Wayne who finally broke the silence. "That was about when the oil business first began to get good. It wasn't long after that when it sure got good. Yes sir, J.P., for a few years the harvest was goddamn sure good, easy pickin', especially when crude got up to around thirty-five bucks. Christ, I almost needed a Wells Fargo truck to carry the night's take to the bank. High rollers were standin' in line waitin' to lay their money on the table. But the bloom's off the rose now. Business has been a drag. My old customers are playing forty-two with their golf partners and sleeping at home with their old ladies. Lots of nights the bartender doesn't take in enough to pay his wages. An' what players come in want to play dollar-limit poker. Shit, play all night to win a hundred bucks. Midland looks like a goddamn ghost town, an' believe me, J.P., money's tighter a nun's cunt."

"Yeah," J.P. agreed. "You can see it here, too. Everybody's playing their cards close to their vest since the bottom's dropped out of oil. Did you come up for the races?"

"Well, that, and I thought I might put the bite on some of my used-to-be regulars who come up here to beat the heat, and I mean heat in more ways than one. It damned sure doesn't take long to change a big spender into a four flushin' deadbeat. I got a pocket full of IOUs I'm going to try to collect. And who knows, while I'm here I might run into a game or two. Must be some action here because there damned sure isn't any anywhere else, short of Vegas or Reno. Anyway, J.P., when I read about you bein' here I figured you'd put me onto a winner or two. Kind of help me pay expenses, you know."

"Well, if I get the word on something good, I'll let you know," J.P. said as he snuffed out his cigarette in the ash tray. "Want some more coffee?"

"That's plenty. When does your horse run again?"

"This comin' weekend. In the Oklahoma Futurity."

"Will it win?"

"Who knows?" J.P. said with a shrug of his shoulders.

"Well, will it run in the money?" Wayne pressed.

"Maybe," J.P. answered with some hesitancy. "The Futurities are run straight. There's no screwin' around, so it's a horse race. Paragon won't be a favorite. He hasn't got that much history behind him. The jockey has a good rep, and is in good standing this season. The handicappers will figure that in. The horse'll probably go onto the tote board with fairly long odds. But personally, I think its got a damned good chance of ending up in the money. Of course I might be accused of showing a little favoritism," he said with a self conscious laugh. "I'm not the only one who thinks the horse has something to offer," J.P. continued. "Mister Trainham told me that an eastern stable approached him yesterday with an offer to buy the horse."

"Would that leave you out in the cold, or have you got another nag or two lined up?" Wayne asked rather indifferently.

"No," J.P. replied. "Trainham turned 'em down. More for sentimental reasons than anything else, I think. He's a rancher who's been around horses all his life. He knows good horse flesh and he's a good horseman, but he's in a different world when it comes to the world of running horses. I don't think he knows what he's got in the horse I'm training. I doubt if he knows what it's worth. From what he told me, I think some son-of-a-bitch is trying to slip up on his blind side wanting to steal the horse."

"Oh?" A noticeable inflection showed that something J.P. had said caught Wayne's interest. "Who is it that's wanting to buy the horse and what kind of an offer did they make?"

J.P. glanced down at his coffee cup, then worked at taking a package of cigarettes from his shirt pocket. He shook out a cigarette, methodically tapped one end of it on the table top several times before lighting up. He looked at

Wayne for some moments before saying: "Dock said that it was the trainer who came to him and made the offer. I don't think you'd know him. The outfit's from back east."

"J.P., for some reason you're weaseling on me," Wayne reproved with a sharp edge to his voice. "What the hell's so secretive about the deal?"

J.P. studied his cigarette as he worried the burning end of it around in the ash tray, meticulously brushing off what little ash that accumulated. Why have I always felt cowed around this son-of-a-bitch, he berated himself introspectively. It's none of his damned business what Scavarda offered Dock, an' I ought to tell him so. But for some fuckin' reason he's always kind of intimidated me. Maybe it's because I know him. I know how dangerous he can be and how it doesn't pay to try and push him around. I'm not afraid of him but I'd sure hate to cross him. And then too, maybe I kowtow to him because he was about the only one who reached down to give me help when I needed it.

He made an effort to meet Wayne's unrelenting, probing eyes, "Well, Dock didn't say as much, but it might be that he'd rather that kind of news wasn't spread around. You know how those kind of deals are?"

"Goddamnit, J.P., you act like you figure me for some fuckin' loudmouth. It doesn't make a rat's ass to me who wants to buy your damned horse. I'm not in the fuckin' horse business. You brought it up, I didn't." Wayne shoved his chair back and rose. "See you around," he growled as he started for the door.

J.P. stood. "Wayne," he called out. The man stopped, his hand on the door handle, his back to the room. "It's always puzzled me how you could be such a cool gambler and yet have such a short fuse hooked to an explosive temper," J.P. said in an attempt to placate with some humor.

"I can control it," Wayne retorted. He turned to face J.P. It just pisses me off for an old friend, one that I've given a hand to when he was wallowing in the gutter with puke on his shirt and piss in his pants, to treat me like I was a goddamn kid that can't be trusted."

"Well," J.P. said, "I know you won't spread it around. It was a fellow named Scavarda, an' he offered Dock eighty grand."

"Find something good for me to bet on," Wayne said as he opened the door and let himself out.

10

Dock stood in the open doorway, blocking much of the early morning sunlight that was the only source of illumination in the windowless horse stall. He had to squint into the shadowy interior to make out the figure of the black man who was bent over a pitchfork piling the soiled straw bedding on a stack near the doorway. "Morning, Tommy," he greeted.

"Mornin' Mister Dock," the man replied as he straightened up from his work.

"Is Paragon on the walker?" Dock inquired.

"No sir. Mister J.P. told me to tell you that he had the horse over to the swimmin' pool," Tommy replied.

"Swimming pool?" Dock questioned.

"Yes sir," Tommy answered. "You know, over there in the barn beside the walker."

"Oh, yeah," Dock replied slowly. After some moments of deliberation, he said rather absently: "Your wife still got the flu bug?"

"Yes sir, but she's some better."

"Don't let that bug get hold of you Tommy. You haven't got time to be sick. We've got too much to do around here," Dock cautioned good naturedly.

"Don't you worry none about that, Mister Dock. I'm sleepin' on the couch. I ain't takin' no chances."

Dock laughed. "That's good. It won't hurt you to sleep by yourself for a few nights. A man can get behind in his homework, but can catch up pretty quick, you know."

Tommy laughed. "You got that right. It wasn't so when I was a young stud. I lusted after that fluff, but I has slowed down considerably."

They laughed. "See you later," Dock said as he turned and headed for the big barn which housed the therapy pool. His pace was hurried. J.P. had not mentioned any problems during their early morning telephone conversation, but maybe something had happened since then. They had never put Paragon in the pool before, and as Dock understood it, it was a therapeutic method for treating lameness.

When he reached the sea-green, metal building he found J.P. leaning nonchalantly against a hitching rail, smoking a cigarette and holding Paragon by a halter shank.

J.P.'s brow knotted as he watched Dock approaching on the graveled pathway. "You're walking like a man with a mission. Something come up?" he asked when Dock came within easy earshot.

"That's what I want to know," Dock said. "Have we got a lame horse?"

"No. What made you think so?"

"Well, Tommy told me that you had him over here. I figured something was wrong."

"There's nothing wrong with Paragon," J.P. replied. "He's top deck."

"Well, you've never put him in the pool before."

"That's right," J.P. replied. "Swimming horses is something new to me. It's come into being while I was, well, while I was semi-retired, you might say," he said with a wry grin. "I've been over here several times looking it over. You're right, it's used some to work out stiffness, or sore muscles. But it's also a good way to exercise horses. The vet tells me it's like swimming for people; it's a good way to exercise muscles that you never knew you had, same way with horses. And he said it's good for their wind, makes 'em breath deep. I thought I'd give it a try. I knew you'd be along after you talked with Tommy, so I was waitin' on you."

"Good. Let's go see what it's all about."

J.P. dropped the cigarette butt and mashed it into the gravel with his boot. Leading the black stallion they entered the coliseum-like barn through double-wide doors. The roof had intermittent, green plastic sections which were translucent and the sides of the barn were spaced with large, sliding glass windows that were open to dispel the heat generated by the summer sun.

In the center of the building was a large, concrete lined pool of aqua blue water, long in length but narrow in width. Gentle graded access slopes were at each end of the pool. An attendant told J.P. and Dock to lead their horse to the east end of the pool. He snapped a second lead shank to the jaw ring of Paragon's halter. With J.P. on one side of the pool holding one lead shank and the attendant positioned on the opposite side with the other lead the two men led the horse up to the lip of the descending ramp. Paragon lowered his head to smell the water. His nostrils flared and he blew the rollers in his nose. He pulled back against the halter ropes. "Easy boy," J.P. soothed. "It ain't gonna hurt ya." He clucked his tongue. "Come on boy." The horse gave to the steady forward pull on the halters. "Dock," J.P. said in a quiet voice. "Why don't you step in behind him and lean your shoulder against his butt. Kinda ease him on."

"You boys got to remember, this horse was raised in West Texas. He's never seen that much water in one place before," Dock said quietly as he stepped in behind the horse.

After two passes through the pool Paragon lost his fear and took to it readily. They led him to swim back and forth, each man on a halter rope, coaching him along. Gradually the attendant increased the pressure of the underwater jets, forcing the horse to exert a greater swimming effort against the strong currents. After four laps J.P. led Paragon over to the drain apron. He held the horse there while the attendant wiped him dry and rubbed him down with a coat conditioner. "Damn," Dock commented from the side line. "That's pampering 'em. I sure hope my ranch horses don't get wind of this kind of horse treatment. They'd probably go out on strike. Best they ever get is a hit an' a lick with a curry comb."

"Mister Dock, J.P., I got somethin' to tell you," Tommy said to the two men as they led Paragon back into his stall.

"What is it, Tommy?" J.P. asked as he pulled the bottom half of the split door to and snapped the lock in place over the hasp.

"I, . . . uh, well, I guess I done got me another job," the black man stammered.

"Got another job! What do you mean, you got another job? What the hell is wrong with this job?" J.P. barked.

"Well, Mister J.P., there's nothin' wrong with workin' here. I sure likes you an' Mister Dock. An' me an that horse, we're not only the same color," Tommy said over a forced laugh, "but we gets along good together. It's just that while you all was gone over to the exercise pool, a couple fellows come by an' offered me more money if I'd go over to their stable. More money than I could turn down."

"Well I'll be go to hell, Tommy," Dock snorted. "How'd you know that I wouldn't meet their offer? You didn't even think to see what I'd do?"

"Mister Dock," Tommy replied without meeting Dock's probing, angry eyes. "They offered to pay me twice what I'm gettin' with you. I sure figured you wouldn't want to double my pay, an' I'd a felt bad about hittin' you up for that kind of money. You'd figure I was lying' to you, tryin' to jack you up."

"What the hell are you gonna do for 'em to earn that kind of money?" J.P. asked, in a voice clipped with anger.

"Well sir, just groom horses, an' the likes. You know, Mister J.P., that's about all I know how to do."

"Who's stable you going to?" J.P. demanded.

"I don't know who owns it, but them fellows said that I'd be workin' for Marvin Yeager, the man what trains for 'em."

J.P. turned to watch Dock slowly nod his head. The two men exchanged knowing looks.

"A man's got to look out for himself, Tommy," Dock said. "I'll go over to the pickup and write you a check. I know you'll do those people a good job, like you've done for us."

"Well shit, Tommy you're leaving us in a helluva bind, you know," J.P. reproved sternly after Dock was out of hearing range. "I don't know where in the hell I can go to find someone to take your place; someone who knows horses, an's reliable enough to keep a safe watch on Paragon."

"J.P., I know I'm leavin' you in a tight," Tommy replied quietly. "I don't want no hard feelin's. I didn't want to say nothin' in front of Mister Dock, 'cause I know he's worried about his horse; worried about someone tryin' to get to him. But listen, J.P., them two fellows wouldn't take no for an answer. I turned 'em down at first, but they just kept raisin' the ante. Finally one of 'em said to me: 'Boy,' an' J.P., you know I hate to be called boy. 'Boy,' he said, 'you'd be stupid to turn our offer down. It'd likely cause you to have a spell of real bad luck. Do you understand me, boy?' he asked. Well I understood all right. A stable hand like me ain't got no business tryin' to stand up against people like that. J.P., I got my family to worry about. I can't pay no rent or buy no groceries if I'm all crippled up. I've seen them kind of musclemen before around the tracks. When they say jump, a little man like me looks at the odds an' asks how high. You understand where I'm comin' from, J.P.?"

"I guess I do. But Tommy, I want to ask you to do something for me. Dock's a decent fellow. He don't understand some of the things that go on around the track. I didn't tell you but these people that you're going to work for have offered to buy Paragon. They made Dock an offer but he turned 'em down. I had it figured that if they wanted the horse bad enough they'd put the screws to him some way. Hiring you is the beginning. I don't think that'll change Dock's mind, so there's no way of telling what they might try next. Will you keep your eyes and ears open over there and let me know if you hear or see anything that might concern us or Paragon?"

"I sure will J.P. Anything I can . . ."

"Here comes Dock," J.P. interrupted. "I don't want him to know about any of this. No need in getting him stirred up and worried any more than he is already."

The Paddock, a popular watering hole in Sierra Vista for horsemen, was bustling with the after five, convivial elbow benders and early diners. Dock and J.P. made their way through the milling crowd, hunting for an empty table in the dimly lighted dining area. They walked the length of the long bar, past the many young people perched on bar stools or crowded in between to gain access to the bar and the young woman serving drinks. The incessant babbling of voices, punctuated by sudden outbursts of light-hearted laughter, drowned out Peter Jenning's reading of the evening news on a TV positioned over the bar beside the mounted head of a eight point buck deer. Waitresses dressed in stylish designer jeans, cowboy boots, and western styled shirts, the in-crowd's attire in Sierra Vista during the racing season, scurried back and forth from the bar or through the swinging doors to the kitchen carrying trays of food and beverages to the dining area. The atmosphere was heavy with the odors of tobacco smoke, brewers' malt and steaks on the grill.

The two horsemen found an unoccupied table in a shadowy corner beside the dormant fireplace. When a harried looking waitress came to clean off the table, Dock ordered a bourbon and branch water and asked for menus. J.P. ordered black coffee.

"I don't think I'm gonna be able to find anyone. Not this late in the season," J.P. said. "Those that are worth a damn already have jobs."

"Well, as I said in the pickup," Dock replied as he nervously drummed his finger tips on the table top, "them hiring Tommy away from us gives me all the more reason to want someone with the horse around the clock."

"I've decided the thing for me to do is to move my bedding over to the barn," J.P. said. "I'll take Tommy's place at night. I can hire some kid to muck out the stall, pack feed, an' those kind of chores. He can stay with Paragon during the day when you or I can't be there. Not too much danger of anyone pulling any shenanigans in broad daylight while people are working around the barn. The rest'll be up to me an' you, if you're willing."

"You know I am," Dock replied. "What do you think that Scavarda bunch is up to?"

"I nosed around some today while I was trying to find a decent hand," J.P. said as he habitually worked a cigarette out of the pack in his shirt pocket. "The word I hear is that old man Scavarda made his money as a union boss. He's one of those people who need to launder some of their income through legitimate businesses, and also needs some tax write-offs. That's probably why he's messing around with a racing stable. It's a good cover, and a person can damned sure turn a lot of green bucks into a lot of tax-deductible green horse shit."

The waitress brought the cocktail, coffee and two menus. The men studied the choices while Dock sampled his highball and J.P. sipped his coffee. The waitress returned to take their orders.

After she picked up the menus and left, Dock leaned across the table and said: "He tried to buy Paragon and I turned him down. Why the hell doesn't he just hunt up another horse? There's bound to be a lot of good horses that could be bought for the kind of money he's willing to fork over."

"I don't know," J.P. replied. "I'm sure that Yeager's watched Paragon run. He's no doubt got some men watchin' and puttin' the stop watch on him when I've had him on the track. Yeager's a horseman, that's for sure. But like you say, there's other good horses here that can be picked up in a claiming race, or bought private treaty. There'll be a big auction here at the end of the season, and a lot of good horses'll go under the hammer."

"Maybe we're hunting boogers," Dock ventured. "Tommy's a good hand. He's a willing worker. You can see that he has a feel and an understanding for horse flesh. You said when you hired him that he had a good reputation. Maybe, like you've found out, there aren't other decent men available, so Scavarda an' Yeager decided to just lay their ears back and hire him away from us. Like you said, it's all a tax write-off."

"That's probably it," J.P. placated. But inwardly, he couldn't buy that. They might have known Tommy was a good man and, not caring about the money, they might have been willing to pay whatever it took to get him. But to strong-arm him into submission? No. There's a helluva lot more at stake here than Tommy's abilities, J.P. thought.

The two men sat, absorbed with their thoughts. Dock finally broke the silence. "J.P., we're bull shittin' each other, an' you know it."

59

J.P. looked up from studying his coffee cup. "I guess we are," he said with deliberation. "For those kind of wages, they could take their pick of just about anybody. Lots of boys as good as Tommy would jump through a hoop for wages like that. The thing is, they knew we were relying on Tommy to be a night watchman and that he's reliable. I think they figured hiring him away from us would accomplish two things: It would show you they mean business, and they have the ways and means to get what they want. What do you think?"

"I think you're right," Dock replied. "They want the horse. Why they're so set on him, I'm not sure. It isn't just because he's a black stallion. They've undoubtedly spent some time studyin' him. They're convinced, just like we are, that he's got the makings of a champion. They see the possibility of cashing in on him, both on the track and as a proven sire. That's what I think."

"That may be, Dock," J.P. agreed. "And remember, his breeding makes him one of a kind. If he proves himself, he's the only source of that particular breeding. He'd be the foundation sire. If he's bred to the right kind of mares and his get prove themselves on the track, shit Dock, he could well be another Leo."

"And I'll tell you something else," Dock said. "People like this Scavarda are used to having things go their way. It probably galled the shit out of him when I turned him down with what he thought was a gold-plated offer to a country hick."

"What does it all add up to?" J.P. asked in a voice that carried deep concern. "You still wantin' to run the race?"

"You damned right! We aren't goin' let 'em scare us off, are we?"

"I'm with you," J.P. replied hastily. A grin slowly replaced the worried frown.

11

Early morning was J.P.'s favorite time of day. He sat on the tack box, smoking a cigarette and enjoying the warmth of the sun as it eased above the horizon to dispel the predawn chill. He glanced over at Paragon eating grain from a rubber tub feeder, watched with idle amusement how the horse used his nose and upper lip to sort through the feed, picking out the choice bits as meticulously as a person might finger through a nut mix hunting for the honey almonds.

He stood and yawned deeply as he walked over to take a lead rope and bridle off a wall peg, then stepped into the horse stall to hook the snap on the end of the lead rope into a ring on Paragon's halter. "Come on, boy," he said as he swung the door open and led the stallion out into the bright sunlight.

J.P. took pleasure in these morning workouts. The temperament of horses and people alike seemed better after a night's rest and in the coolness of a new day. Beads of mountain dew spangled the Kentucky Bluegrass that bordered the graveled walkways leading from the barn area to the paddock and track. The washed air was fragrant with the smell of healthy horses and timothy hay. The plaintive call of a mourning dove added to the at-peace-with-the-world feeling J.P. felt as he lead Paragon toward the track.

The barn area was alive with activities as people went about their chores. Horses were fed and watered in their stalls and then led outside for grooming. Stalls were cleaned and bedded with fresh sawdust. Tack was cleaned and oiled. Farriers were bent over, tacking aluminum racing plates on horses' hooves. Things were being readied for another day of training in preparation for the upcoming weekend racing card. People talked back and forth as they chored—about horses, horse racing, the night life of Sierra Vista, horses and horse racing.

"Morning, J.P. You sure got that colt shining like polished leather. Looks like he's in top form."

"Thanks, Ruben. He's sure a nice colt. Ain't nothin' I can fault about him.

He's got a good mouth, an' gentle as a kitten. You on the card this weekend?"

"Yeah. We're up twice on Thursday, then again one race Saturday and one Sunday."

"You're fielding some top horses this season, Ruben."

"Thanks, J.P., and good luck to you in the Futurity Sunday."

"We'll need all the luck we can get. There'll be some tough competition. See ya, Ruben."

"Take it easy, J.P."

Dock was waiting at the paddock holding the reins on a horse called Flax, a dark palomino gelding with a heavy mane and tail the color of pale-yellow gold. Flax was a leased horse that J.P. used to pony Paragon during the warm-up sessions. J.P. took Flax's reins from Dock, stuck the toe of his left boot into the stirrup and raised himself to step across the horse's back. He picked up the off-side stirrup with his right foot and settled himself into the stock saddle. "I'll ease Paragon around for a while," he said. "He's a little stiff from his swimming yesterday. It's about seven thirty now. Sonny said he'd be here a little after eight. Dock, why don't you see if you can line up a gate handler for about eight. We'll time him at a furlong an' a half." He dallied Paragon's lead rope around the saddle horn and started out at an easy walk onto the freshly-harrowed oval track.

There were already a number of horses on the track. Some, like Paragon, were being ponied and some were being ridden at various gaits by exercise people riding flat saddles. J.P. moved along easy on Flax, with Paragon crowding his right side. The black colt was fresh and filled with the excitement of being in the company of other horses. He nickered and pranced as he fought at the restraining halter shank that held him to a walk.

Flax was an old hand at ponying young, spirited horses. About the only signal he needed from a man on his back was a stop or go cue. The palomino had a rocking chair rhythm to his gait that could easily lull a rider into a wool-gathering state. J.P. glanced up to see where the sun stood. Well, he thought. Lynn's probably still in bed an' I imagine Virginia's workin' her tail off serving a house full of customers.

Seeing them again in his mind's eye, the bittersweet memories of their lives together, brought a constriction to J.P.'s throat and a wave of longing. Like the longing that met him each evening when he opened the door to a dark and silent house. Like the longing and the ache that came with the hearing of their favorite song. Like the longing he would awaken to when he reached across the bed for Virginia and she wasn't there. He shook his head in self-reproach. "Flax," he said to the horse which flicked its ears at the sound of its name, "I've learned a few things in my life, mostly the hard way." But, he thought, I guess the most important thing I've learned is that the greatest thing in life is to love someone and to have their love in return. That's more important to me than all the money that floats around this track. The trouble is, a person doesn't realize that until he's had it and let it slip away from him. "But if I get 'em back, I'll never let 'em down again," he said aloud.

The thoughts of Virginia and Lynn brightened J.P.'s spirits. He let his mind dwell and fantasize on the possibility of having them back, and what it would mean to his life. The nostalgia subsided and was replaced by the probability of a better day coming. A day that might be almost within reach. Virginia had said in her last letter that she still loved him and that she and Lynn missed him.

J.P. loosened the halter and slipped the snaffle bit into Paragon's mouth while Sonny was tightening the cinch of his racing saddle. "The track boss said we could use the starting gate and he'd have the track cleared for us at nine thirty," J.P. told Sonny. "Dock's got the gate men lined up. We've never had any real trouble gettin' Paragon to take the gate but we've never tried to load him without other horses at the post. So Dock's gonna put Flax in the gate right beside the one you'll use. I think he'll take it that way without any trouble. Anyway, Dock'll be there to help in case you have a problem. I'll put the clock on you at the three hundred and thirty yard post. As you know, Paragon runs better against another horse. He tends to loaf a bit without competition so you'll probably need to go to your bat before you cover the distance. I don't see anyone hangin' around who might want to run a clock on him so I want you to bring him right along. Let's see what he'll do this morning, O.K.?"

"You got it," Sonny replied as he buckled the chin strap to his crash helmet.

J.P. stepped up beside the black horse and gave Sonny a leg up to set him astraddle the horse. "Oh," J.P. injected, "I almost forgot. What'd you weight in at this morning?"

"Hundred and twelve," Sonny replied. "I'm gettin' fat. I'm going to have to go on a diet," he said as he picked the rein up and rode Paragon away from the paddock toward the big green starting gate which set across a tangent at the northeast end of the oval track.

J.P. crossed over to the grandstand side of the track. He would wait at the three hundred and thirty yard marker with a stopwatch in one hand and a red flag in the other. Dock would be standing beside the starting gate with a stopwatch and a flag. When the gate swung open, Dock would activate his watch and signal the starting time with a downward sweep of his flag. That would alert J.P. to start his watch. When Sonny jockeyed Paragon across the finish line in front of him, J.P. would stop his watch and mark the end of the run for Dock by a motion of his flag. The two men would then compare their watches and take the average as the time for the run.

J.P. was intent on watching the proceedings at the post. He did not hear nor see the man who walked up behind him.

"That your horse in the gate?"

"J.P. turned to see who had spoken. "Oh, hello Wayne. You're out early."

"Yeah, this mountain air makes a man feel alive. 'Specially after a hot summer in Texas. You fixin' to run your horse against the clock?"

"Yeah."

As he saw Dock's arm sweep downward with a white handkerchief, J.P. pushed the stem on his stop watch. He watched Paragon come charging out of the starting gate, Sonny bent low over the horse's neck, urging him on. He saw Sonny go to the bat. Paragon responded. Ears laid back and head thrust forward—a living wedge driving a hole in the clean mountain air, trailing a dusty wake.

It was a picture of pure grace and beauty. Man and beast in perfect harmony. Muscular actions rippling the jet black coat. Legs moving in rhythmic coordination, reaching out in sequence to claim a piece of turf and thrust it, and a little tuft of red dirt, behind. J.P.'s mouth turned dry and his hands clammy as he watched the horse eat up the distance that separated them. Sonny seemed to float above the horse, boots in the stirrups, his legs doubled under him and his upper body crunching parallel to Paragon's back and thrusting neck. Horse and man were as one as they thundered past. A seizure of excitement gripped J.P. in the gut as he swept his arm down signaling the end of the run and his thumb set the time on the stopwatch.

"Goddamn, man that black bastard can run a lick," Wayne said.

"He's got foot," J.P. agreed as he stole a look at the watch. "He's a helluva colt," he said through a grin that crowded past the intended serious demeanor.

"What's his time?" Wayne asked.

J.P. did not respond. He dropped the watch into his shirt pocket, buttoned the pocket flap and then rolled the red flag up on the staff.

"What was his time?" Wayne asked again, irritation edging his voice.

"Wayne," J.P. said very slowly. "In your line of work you don't advertise your hole card. In my line of work my horse's runnin' time is my hole card."

Wayne snorted. "All right you tight-fisted, son-of-a-bitch," he said with a forced laugh. "I'll get you across the table from me in a card game one of these days an' when I do, don't think I won't remember."

"If I'm playing in your back yard," J.P. responded, "I'll expect to play by your rules. OK?"

"Yeah, I understand. I was just curious," Wayne replied with a tone of irritation edging his voice.

Sonny rose to a half stand, his weight in the stirrups. He exerted gentle pressure on the snaffle bit and brought Paragon to an easy trot after the run. At the west side of the track he turned the horse around and posting, started back towards the gate leading off the track to the paddock. Dock was riding Flax in from the opposite direction.

"You told me a fellow named Trainham owns the horse," Wayne said as J.P. started to walk away.

J.P. stopped and turned part way around to reply. "Yeah, Dock Trainham."

"He owns a ranch over south of Midland, don't he?"

"Yeah," J.P. replied after several moments hesitation. "Down near a place called Horsehead Crossing." J.P. turned to continue toward the paddock.

"I want to meet him," Wayne said and moved along to walk beside J.P. The color rose in J.P.'s face, his neck stiffened and he clenched his jaws in suppressed anger at Wayne's overbearing insolence. From a longstanding acquaintance J.P. knew that Wayne's interest in a person was seldom without an ulterior, self-serving motive.

Dock had dismounted and was slipping the halter on Paragon while Sonny was loosening the saddle cinch. Dock asked over his shoulder, "What did you clock him at?" When J.P. failed to answer, he turned to look at him. He saw Wayne standing beside his trainer. Sonny slipped his saddle off and said: "I'll go put my gear away, change my boots and will see you all over at the barn."

"OK, Sonny," J.P. said.

Dock looked at Wayne who was walking slowly around Paragon, studying the horse's conformation.

"I don't believe we've met," Dock said as Wayne came around to stand in front of the horse.

"Uhh," J.P. faltered, then yielded. "Dock Trainham, this is Wayne Belcheff. He runs a private club over in Midland. I've known him for a number of years."

"Pleased to meetcha," Dock said. The two men extended their hands in a sociable gesture. Dock noted the soft looking hand with manicured nails and an impressive gold ring. He accepted the man's hand, expecting one of those dead-fish handshakes but winced as the sudden pain in his own limp hand from Wayne's hard grip took him by surprise. Dock firmed up his own grip to counter. He looked closer to reappraise this dude-looking fellow. Black hair, graying in the sideburns under the brim of an expensive Stetson and a black, neatly-trimmed mustache were prominent against the indoor pallor of the man's complexion. But the striking feature, the feature that Dock would always associate with Wayne Belcheff, were his eyes. Hard and cold, like gray chert. Eyes that belied the man's easy smile. Dock sensed that the man was sizing him up, looking for an advantage, something vulnerable. The smile faded from Dock's features.

"I've heard of you," Wayne said.

"Well, I wouldn't know how," Dock replied cautiously. "I seldom go to Midland. That's an oilman's town. I do my business in Pecos. That's a cowman's town."

"I know your boy, Pat," Wayne replied, his eyes studying Dock's face for the reaction.

"Oh?" Dock puzzled. "You might be talking about my stepson, Patrick. He's been working in the oil patch around Odessa and Midland."

"That's who I'm talkin' about," Wayne said.

A shadow of uncertainty and concern clouded Dock's features.

12

Sonny sat on the redwood bench, his back against the wall, eyes closed and his jaw slack in that somnolent state just short of sleep. The sound of the sauna door opening and closing roused him. Swirling clouds of steam rose from the pit of hot rocks in the center of the small room, fading the brilliancy of the overhead light to a muted orange.

"Hey, Rogers, you in here?" a voice called.

"Yeah," Sonny replied lethargically. He swiped at his face with a towel to wipe the stinging sweat from his eyes. He squinted at the approaching figure but could only make out a white towel wrapped around the midriff of a brown, naked body coming toward him through the heavy mist. "That you Rodriquez?" he asked as the fellow jockey began to take form in front of him.

"Yeah, it's me. Was you expecting maybe Bo Derek?"

"Do I have a choice?" Sonny drawled.

Lalo Rodriquez doubled his bath towel and spread it on the bench. He took up the bucket of water and walked over to douse the hot rocks. He paused to watch the steam billow above the fire pit then turned and walked back to sit gingerly on his towel. "Did you ever get laid in the steam bath?" he asked as he closed his eyes and eased back against the hot wall.

"No, have you?"

"No, but I got laid once in a hot tub," Lalo said. "Man, it was hell tryin' to keep things where they belonged. My ass kept wantin' to float to the top like a cork." Both men laughed.

"I've been lookin' for you, Rogers. I'm dating a chick who's got a friend who wants to meet you."

"Yeah?" Sonny replied unenthusiastically.

"Yeah. The babe I'm charging is going to have a party over at her place tonight. She asked me to bring you along."

"Lalo," Sonny said in a lazy voice, "you apprentice jockeys have a lot to learn before you get track-wise. Let an old hand give you some advice. Sure, some of these track followers will give you the come-on. They'll play around with you, baitin' you on for inside tips on the races. When they're tired of the game, they'll pat you on the head like you were some damned kid, kiss you on the forehead and go cozy up to some son-of-a-bitch that's flashing a bankroll and driving a Mercedes. Everything's relevant, Lalo. It's all relevant. Relevant to money, that is, with these track broads." Sonny rose and stretched. "See you around." He picked up his towel and wrapped it around his middle, taking a tuck to bind it. "Lalo, I'm like the dog making love to a skunk. I've had about all this pleasure I can stand. Give my thanks to your girl friends but tell 'em my social calendar's booked for this month."

"Wait a minute," Lalo said as he sat upright. "Man, these girls ain't that way. These girls got class. Let me clue you in on this deal."

"All right," Sonny said reluctantly and sat back down. "I'm sure you've run into a couple of high-class virgins."

"I met this chick a couple nights ago," Lalo said. "Let me tell you, her kind don't run in bunches. She drives a fire-engine-red Corvette convertible. An' man, she's got this neat condo back up in the hills. She thinks horses are cute and jockeys are macho, you know?"

"Yeah, I know and you and your track tramps aren't raisin' my blood pressure any," Sonny replied.

"Tramp? No way, man," Lalo protested. "They got a box in the Jockey Club."

"Well, if they're that well-heeled, why in hell would they want to meet me? And what the hell are they doing palling around with a pecker-headed Mexican like you?" Sonny pressed.

"Man, they think I'm the next Eddie Arcaro. But, shit if I know why they want to hook up with some old fart like you. I told my chick to tell her friend that Rogers ain't got no class," Lalo said through a good-natured laugh. "But she says her friend owes you a favor. She'd cashed in some win tickets with long odds on your mounts. Hell, man, get smart. Maybe she wants to mount you on something to even the score."

"I think you're full of shit," Sonny said as he stood up.

"Hey man, it's gonna be a swingin' party," Lalo said. "This chick I'm chargin' is a good looking bitch. Got a set of knockers like Dolly Parton."

"Yeah," Sonny replied, "and this blind date you're tryin' to palm off on me, on a scale of one to ten, will class at a minus three."

The two men laughed. "Man, you know thoroughbreds don't run with broom tails," Lalo persisted. "Barbara, that's my chick, she told me to tell you that you won't be disappointed. Shit, man, this is our last night to howl before a long weekend. You don't want to sit on your ass by yourself watchin' the fuckin' TV, do you?"

"All right," Sonny yielded reluctantly. "Where and what time?"

"As soon as we get out of here I'm supposed to call Barbara," Lalo replied. "She an' her friend'll meet us at the Paddock. They're gonna take us up to White Mountain Inn for a bite to eat. Then we're gonna lay around the pool. You gringos can get a sun tan so you'll look like me," he said with a laugh. "See, man, you can take a trial run. If you don't like what you see, an' you'll sure as hell see most of the merchandise, you can duck out."

The bar was dark and cool, easy on the eye after the intense glare of the midday sun in downtown Sierra Vista. A psychedelic juke box lit up a dark corner giving forth Willie Nelson's rendition of "Sweet Georgia Brown," a subtle background for the drone of voices and occasional outbursts of laughter. Patrons, mostly track people, were perched on bar stools nursing Bloody Marys or beer. Lalo and Sonny selected a table off to one side but near the front entrance where the girls would see them.

Lalo was saying something about his mounts for the upcoming racing days as they eased into chairs, but Sonny only heard the words in a perfunctory way. His thoughts were on his commitment to the uncertainty of a blind date and his regret for going against his better judgment. Especially a date arranged by Lalo, a swaggering, impressionable kid to whom the wearing of the silks was an ego trip. Some track-happy broad gives him the come on, figuring to get a handle on a winner or two, and this pecker-head thinks she's on the make for him, Sonny thought. I don't know why the hell I let him talk me into this. Maybe I can come up with some excuse and duck out later this afternoon.

At thirty-four, Sonny was in the autumn of the expected good years for jockeying. The concern over what he would do when he passed his prime was beginning to be a cause for apprehension. The thought of being relegated to anything around the track less than being a jockey was unacceptable. And to work anywhere but around horses and racing people would be slow death.

His size, for as far back as he could remember, had always been a disadvantage, an emotional problem. How many scuffles had he had in the school yard over boys calling him peewee, or shorty? How many times had he sat frustrated in the bleachers in school watching other boys earn their letter sweaters and the cheers of girls? How many times had he found something else to do during scheduled school dances rather than face the embarrassment of dancing with a girl taller than he was, or standing in a corner wishing he were somewhere else? But yet he was driven from the backwaters by an inner compulsion to excel; to prove himself an equal, or maybe better. On his eighteenth birthday he had tried to enlist in the Marines so he could join the fighting men in Vietnam. The recruiting sergeant had told him he did not meet the physical requirements—underweight and too small.

It had been that necessity to stand as an equal in a manly occupation that led him to the race track and horses. He had started out as an exercise boy. The unrelenting inner drive and self-discipline drove him to develop the stamina, the strength and the balance necessary for the mastery of horsemanship, the requisites of a good jockey. He contended against the field with perseverance, hard work and integrity to become one of the top-rated jockeys in the southwest.

The adrenalin-producing sensation of balancing atop an eleven hundred pound horse running full tilt in a crowded field, driving to be the first across the finish line. The wearing of the silk, the acclamation and the pot of gold. The ambition and strength of purpose that drove Sonny to push a mount to its limit, or beyond. The rush of the wind against his face and the shouts and cheers from the grandstand as he raced down the stretch. The exhileration of being led into the winner's circle by the proud owner, the horseshoe garland of roses, the winner's blanket, the flash of the photographer's camera, seeing his name in print. In these things Sonny Rogers found his niche, his attainment, a place where he stood shoulder to shoulder with any man—or maybe a cut above.

But when he was away from the track and horses he stood at five-four, in high-heeled cowboy boots. He had to look up at people and he knew that they looked down at him, except when he was in the world of the horse.

Her name was Catherine, but her friends called her Cathy and would Sonny please call her Cathy. She was, Sonny decided, what the ads for women's clothing called petite. Brown hair worn straight, cut square across her forehead and short in back framed an attractive, friendly, suntanned face. Blue mascara backgrounded dark eyes that seemed to never stay set on one place for very long, but flitted from one object to another like a hummingbird in a flower garden. She had a strong mouth and full lips, made sensual by a discreet application of pale pink lipstick.

Sonny lost some of his misgivings about this blind date arrangement as they eased into an acquaintance, visiting about general amenities. He felt much better when the four of them rose to leave the lounge and he found that Cathy stood no taller than he did.

They crowded into Barbara's Corvette and headed south out of Sierra Vista. They traveled the highway that coursed up a narrow mountain valley alongside a calendar-picture stream of crystal clear water, chortling as it frolicked its way between grassy banks and over granite boulders. Up beyond the foothills, up where the blue spruce and long needle pines grew shoulder to shoulder, they drove into a valley that opened wide to embrace a large meadow and the baronial White Mountain Inn with its championship golf course and a lake lying in the grassy cirque like a tear-shaped emerald held in a light green mounting.

As they walked through the impressive lobby amid guests in tourists' togs and expensive western wear, Sonny felt the pressure of self-consciousness eroding his composure. He took some comfort from Cathy when she put her arm through his and walked at his side among the diamonds and the hand-crafted boots like a Thoroughbred filly parading with her jockey to the post on Kentucky Derby Day.

They lunched on the terrace beside the main dining room overlooking the third tee of the golf course and the boat dock. In the stillness of the afternoon the picturesque lake mirrored the towering Apache Peak which reigned over her surroundings like a Queen Mother. Small talk between the four of them centered mostly around Barbara and Cathy's naive questions about horses, horse racing and the lifestyle of a jockey. Lalo swelled and his ego manifested as he answered the girls' questions, expounding and exaggerating. Sonny listened, and smiled inwardly. Lalo, he thought, your as full of shit as a Christmas goose.

After a leisurely lunch, for which Cathy, overriding Sonny's offer and objections, insisted on paying the bill saying that she would just charge it to her room, they decided to adjourn to the pool. Sonny watched as Cathy accepted the check from the waitress and signed it. The realization that she had a room here, a place that he had always considered to be strictly for monied people, people beyond his class, was disturbing. "Let me leave the tip," he offered.

"All right," she agreed as she looked up and smiled.

The two men had changed in the locker room and were waiting at poolside, stretched out in lounging chairs when the girls came walking across the manicured lawn which separated the hotel proper from the swimming pool.

"Hey, man, didn't I tell you you wouldn't be sorry?" Lalo said as they watched the women approach.

Sonny did not bother to reply. From her painted toenails to the little diamond studs in her ear lobes, this Catherine was all class. She wore a one piece, abbreviated white swim suit that left little to the imagination. She smiled and waved. Sonny waved back, and in spite of the deep-rooted caution he harbored about women, his pulse skipped a beat and his hands on the arm rests of the lounge chair were suddenly clammy.

They swam and played in the pool, Sonny shy and hesitant, Cathy aggressive. They stood beside the chaise lounges, shivering in the cool mountain air until the sun warmed away the goose bumps. Lying on their stomachs, their heads cradled on folded arms, they talked in drowsy, muffled voices. As their friendship developed, Sonny's curiosity was piqued about this pretty woman and her background. But she gave him no openings. In fact, she carefully avoided any line of conversation that might lead to her personal life. And she never offered so much as a hint about any interest in his life beyond the track.

Barbara's condominium sat among dark pines on the brink of an escarpment overlooking the scattered lights of the village. Sonny, by force of will, fought down the feeling of inferiority that threatened to engulf him as he parked his pickup among the luxury and sporty cars in the driveway.

Cathy had told him she would arrive early and help Barbara set the stage for the party, and she would meet him there. It was she who answered the chimes, opened the door and greeted him with a smile and a light, unexpected kiss on the cheek. Sonny stepped back half a step to look at her. She was a striking woman in subtle but effective makeup, styled hair and an expensive-looking beige cocktail dress. This is a classy filly and I'm not sure what her motives are, but right now I don't really care, he thought. He let his eyes wander to her full lips that framed perfect white teeth, down to the cleavage which dipped into the top of her dress, down to the slim waist and to the shapely legs and trim ankles.

He glanced at the small group of guests, casually visiting and laughing over their cocktails. He noticed the women's jewelry and expensive clothing and the men with their blazer jackets and hand-lasted, ostrich-skin boots.

Cathy put her arm through his. "Come on," she whispered, "remember, I'm yours and you're mine."

13

The tone of the voice from the other end of the phone line that said "Hello," was not a good start for Dock's day. It was J.P.'s voice, but slurred and thickened. Without waiting for an acknowledgement, J.P. went on: "Dock, you might think it's none of my goddamned business, but I damned sure think it is."

"What the hell are you talking about?" Dock flared at the implication of J.P.'s thick-tongued accusation. The thought of being so dependent on a man who had a history of turning to the bottle in times of stress had, from the beginning, been a disquieting worry to Dock.

"I think you damned well know what I'm talkin' 'bout," J.P. growled. "I'm talkin' 'bout you makin' a deal on Paragon. Dealin' behind my back."

"J.P., I don't. . . ." Dock tried to respond.

"The goddamn horse may be yours, but goddamn it, I've got a helluva lot of my time an' sweat tied up in that colt. You know goddamned well that without me, Paragon wouldn't be where he's at," J.P. ranted. "I've. . . ."

It was Dock's turn to override the conversation. "J.P.," he said in a bridled but tight voice, "you've been drinking."

"You goddamn right I've been drinkin'. Why the hell not, when a man you thought was your best friend stabs you in the back?"

Dock clenched his jaws in exasperation as he listened to the tirade. He breathed in deeply and exhaled slowly, trying to control his temper. His hand holding a death grip on the phone receiver trembled, his stomach knotted and he felt the anger rise up his neck to flush his face. "Where're you at?" he snapped.

"I'm at the track," came the surly reply.

"Have you checked Paragon this morning?" Dock asked, but hating to, dreading the anticipated answer as the knot in his gut grew tighter at the thought of J.P. drinking the night away in some bar, leaving the horse unattended.

"Yeah, I checked him. You may sell out on me, but I for one, sure live up to my end of a deal. I spent the night with your fuckin' horse. That's what I'm paid to do, ain't it?"

A feeling of relief came over Dock. His mind probed for an explanation to J.P.'s unexpected hostility. But as long as the horse was all right, the other matter could, no doubt, be resolved some way or other. "J.P., what the hell's eating on you?" he asked in a conciliatory voice, his disappointment in the man and his anger tempered by the fact that although for some foolish reason J.P. had fallen off the wagon, he had stayed with the horse. There was still an overriding sense of loyalty, so maybe all was not lost.

"I'll tell you what's eatin' on me, you dealin' with Scavarda behind my back," J.P. mumbled, his thickened tongue slurring over the name. "You not thinkin' 'nuff 'bout me to even discuss it with me. That's what the hell's eatin' on me," he mimicked in a voice meant to be insolent.

Dock caught the disrespect. But for the sake of trying to arrive at a peaceful settlement, and not lose his trainer at this crucial time, he chose to let it pass without the rebuke it deserved. "J.P.," he said with studied patience, "I don't know what you mean when you say I'm dealing with Scavarda, especially when you accuse me of dealing behind your back. I've never met the man, much less had dealings with him. And I've damned sure told you all the details of my talks with Yeager. What the hell more is there?" Dock asked, his rising and edgy voice reflecting a slackening of the rein he held on his temper.

Dock's retort registered in J.P.'s fogged mind. It noticeably cooled his hostile attitude as he replied defensibly: "Dock, the word goin' 'round the backside yesterday was that Paragon would be standin' at stud in New Jersey come the end of the meet here. I figured you'd made a deal to sell to Scavarda."

"I'll meet you at the barn in a few minutes," Dock said. "Do you understand? I'll be at the barn as soon as I can get there. You be there."

J.P. was sitting on the tack box under the overhang that fronted the horse stalls. The symptoms of a man-sized hangover were obvious. His hand, as it lifted the cigarette to his mouth, trembled as if he had palsy. The eyes that looked up at Dock's approach were bloodshot and droopy. Dock's rancor subsided some when he saw his horse stick its head over the bottom half of the stall door, dribbling grain from the morning feeding.

"He's eatin' good this morning," J.P. offered as he stood to crush out the half smoked cigarette.

"Good," Dock replied in an even voice. "Now, J.P.," he said in studied patience as he turned his attention from the horse to confront his trainer, "tell

74

me what the hell put the burr under your tail?"

The Irish in J.P. bristled for a moment, trying to recapture the mood of justifiable anger. But the queasy feeling in the pit of his stomach, the dull, throbbing headache behind his eyeballs, the lingering taste of vomit and the stern countenance and steady, steely glare from his employer deflated him. His guilt was amplified by an unbidden feeling of remorse as he stood like an errant child awaiting a sure-to-come whipping. "Well," he finally said with deliberation, "like I told you on the phone. I heard that you made a deal on Paragon. Sold him. I got a lot ridin' on that horse, Dock. I've put a lot into him. If he goes to Scavarda, I'm out. You and Paragon are the way back for me. Both as a trainer and as a man tryin' to get his family back together again."

"J.P.," Dock reprimanded slowly, "like it says in the Good Book, you lack the faith of the mustard seed, thinking I'd sell out without taking you into account. I thought we had a better understanding than that. As far as you running to the bottle, that's your problem. And J.P., I'm gonna tell you flat out, I've already figured out how I'll handle the problem next time. Come hell or high water, you pull that stunt on me again and you can damn sure roll your bed and move on down the road. Do you understand me?"

"I understand, and I wouldn't blame you," J.P. answered sheepishly.

"Go home. Sober up. Get some sleep," Dock ordered. "I'll take care of things around here. Be back here before sundown."

"Dock," J.P. said, "I'd. . . ."

"Go do what I told you to do," Dock interrupted. "And get it out of your head that I made any kind of deal with Scavarda. I don't know what's behind the rumor you heard. We'll talk about it when you're in better shape."

"I had Paragon over on the walker, like I do every afternoon," J.P. said. "Buddy Tally, he works for the Buena Suerte outfit, was there with a horse. While the horses were on the walker we were sittin' in the shade, chewin' the fat. He asked me if I was going back east after the season was over here. I told him no, likely I'd be stayin' on with you and Paragon. We'd probably either put him on the track at Sunland Park or take him back to the ranch for the winter. 'Well,' Buddy said, 'I heard that Paragon was moving to a stable back in New Jersey.'"

"J.P.," Dock cut in, "you've been around long enough to know that there's about as much bull shit floatin' around the track as there is horse shit in the stalls. I don't know where that rumor came from, or the basis for it. All I know is that I told you I had made up my mind not to accept the offer from Scavarda, that Paragon is not for sale. Do I strike you as the kind of man who won't stay hitched to a decision, or whose word isn't worth a damn?"

J.P. fished a cigarette out of a pack, crumpled the empty container and walked over to deposit it in the trash barrel which stood beside the stall door. "Dock," he said after he had lit the cigarette, his voice and demeanor reflecting a feeling of regret and guilt, "I'm sorry. In more ways than one, I'm sorry. You ought to run my ass off. But I hope you'll accept my apology and let me stay on."

"Let's let bygones be bygones," Dock said, "and get on with things that matter."

"I sure hope Virginia don't hear about me tying one on." J.P. mumbled. "It might make her change her mind about giving me a another chance."

"She won't hear it from me," Dock replied, "but J.P., as a friend, I'm gonna tell you that you'd better think long and hard about your drinking problem. If you're going to bury your head in a bottle of booze every time you hit a snag or the going gets a little tough, you'll never hold it together. You know what I'm saying, don't you."

"I know, Dock. Don't think I haven't been kickin' by ass over last night. Buddy telling me that Paragon was goin' back east sure upset me. I stewed about it all the rest of the afternoon. I even went to the phone down at the corner of the barn and tried to call you. But the hotel clerk said that you'd left with another fellow and didn't leave no word. That made me doubly suspicious. Then when I opened the grain box to get the evening feed and found the bottle of Jack Daniels you'd stashed there, it was too tempting. 'Course, I figured to just have one drink, just to kinda brace me up a little, you know. But shit, I know better than that, there's so such thing as one drink for me."

"Are you saying that I put a bottle of whiskey in the feed box?" Dock asked over a frown. "J.P., don't make matters worse by lying. If you bought a bottle, for God's sake be man enough to own up to it."

"Dock, you gotta believe me," J.P. pleaded. "That wasn't my bottle. I haven't bought a bottle of booze since I went to work for you and swore off. I figured it was yours. Jack Daniels is your brand, isn't it?"

The two men stood looking at each other, absorbed with the implications of what they were saying, each taking measure of the degree of veracity of the other. Dock finally broke the silence: "The grain box is supposed to be kept locked. You and I are the only ones with keys."

"I keep it locked. It was locked when I got into it last evening," J.P. responded. "And that bottle of Jack Daniels wasn't there yesterday morning when I fed. Whoever put it there put it there sometime yesterday."

"You say it wasn't your bottle," Dock studied, "and it damned sure wasn't mine. Somebody came by here when they knew we'd both be gone, picked the lock and planted a bottle of my brand of whiskey for you to trip over."

"And they set me up with that wild tale about Paragon going to an eastern syndicate," J.P. snorted. "The sons-of-bitches! An' dumb ass me fell right into their little trap.

"Well, Dock, I'm sorry as hell. But believe me, it won't happen again."

"I told you I didn't think Scarvada was used to the idea of having his offers refused," Dock said. "I suspect he's tightening the screws on us. Them hiring Tommy, leaving us short-handed, was just the beginning. They figured this deal might split us up. Leave me in a lurch. Well, it didn't work. But it tipped their hand. Now we know to keep an eye peeled their way. Once bitten, twice wary; but can just the two of us cover all the bases?"

14

"I didn't order that," the young man said when the bartender set a bottle of beer in front of him. "I haven't finished this one yet."

"Fellow sittin' over there at that table bought it for you," the man behind the bar responded as he pointed to a man at a corner table.

The young man turned on his stool and peered into the smoky, dimly lit lounge to see his benefactor. The man at the table waved him over. He hesitated a moment, then picked up his glass and the bottle of beer and threaded his way through the crowded room to stand beside the corner table.

"Hello, Pat. Sit down."

"Hi, Wayne. Thanks for the beer."

"My pleasure. Drink hearty."

The young man placed his drink on the table, pulled a chair out and sat down. "You here for the races?" he asked.

"A mixed bag of pleasure and business," Wayne Belcheff replied. "What are you doing in Sierra Vista?"

"Well, we just got here yesterday," the young man replied.

"That your girl friend sittin' next to you at the bar?"

Patrick Trainham busied himself carefully pouring beer from the bottle into a tilted glass. He watched the suds slowly rise to crown the glass. "Yeah," he replied without looking up.

"Invite her over. I'll buy her a drink," Wayne suggested.

"Naw, she's all right," Patrick countered. "Anyway, I can't stay. I just came over to see who bought me a beer. It's dark in here, an' I wasn't sure who you were."

Wayne reached into the pocket of his silk sport shirt and pulled out a package of cigarettes. He shook one part way out, reached across the table and offered it to Patrick. The young man accepted it without comment. Wayne shook one out for himself. They both went about lighting up.

"Well, nice to see you," Patrick said as he shoved his chair back away from the table. "Guess I'll be gettin' on back to the bar."

"Wait just a minute," Wayne said with a touch of authority edging his voice. "We've got some unfinished business we need to discuss."

Patrick stopped midway in rising from his chair. He hesitated and looked at the older man. The unsmiling face and the coldness in the eyes of the Texas gambler were enough to convince Patrick that he was not meant to have a choice. He slowly sat back down.

"Pat, I'm holding a fist full of your IOUs," Wayne said. "I've been holding them for a long time. Too damned long. Especially since you've never made an effort to pay a lousy dime on 'em. I guess you think you can walk into my club, run up a big debt and just walk away, scot-free."

The point blank accusation, the dreaded dunning, visibly unnerved the young man. The hand holding the burning cigarette trembled slightly and his eyes grew furtive. "Well," he said hesitantly, "most of what I owe you is gamblin' debts, and gambling is against the law in Texas."

Wayne looked at him for a long moment, a small smile working at the corners of his mouth, as if he relished the contest. "Don't go to crawfishin' on me," he said. "And don't pull that fuckin' Philadelphia lawyer bull shit on me either. We're not talking about what's legal or illegal. We're talking about witnessed promissory notes you signed. Notes substantiating loans. Those notes are legit, my boy."

The two men sat in studied silence. The older man's unblinking eyes staring down the younger man's attempt to meet him head on. It was Wayne who finally spoke: "Don't even think about trying to beat me out of it," his measured words accentuated by the underlying threat. "You're not the first deadbeat I've had to deal with. I've collected from some who were sure enough tough, and believe me, punk, I'll collect from you, one way or another."

"I'm not tryin' to beat you out of what I owe, it's just that the drillin' company laid me off, an' I'm broke," Patrick stammered. "I'll sure pay you Wayne, soon's I can find me a job."

A look of contempt passed over Wayne's features, revealing his disdain for fools. His right hand rested on the table, his fingers methodically drumming out a tattoo and his left hand slowly rotating the whiskey glass. The nattily dressed, impeccably groomed man looked with obvious distaste at the younger man's dirty clothes, his unshaven face and at his shaggy, shoulder-length blond hair which framed weak but rather good-looking features. Wayne shook his head slowly from side to side and said: "Pat, I had you pegged as a spoiled kid, a damned know-it-all, from the very first night you were in the club. I make my living by judging people, an' I seldom make a mistake."

Patrick looked up from studying the beer bottle in front of him. He tried to muster a glare at Wayne over the insulting remark. But the gambler's cold bearing bested him. He dropped his eyes to concentrate on snuffing out his cigarette.

"Somewhere you got the bright idea that you were a card player," Wayne continued. "You probably won a hand or two in the doghouse, playing poker with your roughneck friends. Then you decided to come to town to pick up some easy money from us town dudes. It took me about three hands at the poker table to peg you. From there on you were my pigeon. I just baited you along. I let you win that first night, remember? You were easy picking, Trainham, easy money."

"How much do I owe you?" Patrick asked in a faltering voice.

"A little over ten grand," Wayne replied.

"Ten thousand! Shit fire!" Patrick exclaimed as he braced up to look at Wayne in disbelief. "I didn't think it was near that much."

"Well, you were a smart-ass, an' most of the time you were so high on booze or drugs that you didn't know if you were playing rummy or poker. And maybe you forgot, Trainham, but those notes are carrying twenty per cent interest," Wayne said between the acts of lighting another cigarette. "With thirty dollar crude you oil field people figured you'd never see another poor day. Money was easy come, easy go. Well, crude fell out of bed and now all you high rollers are livin' on unemployment compensation, or maybe like you, spongin' off your old man. That means that my business is a little slow, Trainham, and I'm not running a charity outfit. So I'm callin' in my notes."

"Man, I can't come up with no ten thousand dollars," Patrick protested. "I haven't worked in six months."

The look of disgust faded from Wayne's face and in its place slipped a mask of calculating hostility. He leaned over the table towards the younger man. "Don't hand me that bull shit, you chicken-livered bastard," he growled. "When you were so eager to sign chits right and left, you told me not to worry, that your old man was Dock Trainham who owned the Trainham Ranch west of Odessa. You said he'd cover your losses. Yeah, I checked on your story. Found that he'd bailed you out of messes most of your worthless life. I also found out that you're his only living kin and that you're heir to your mother's estate.

"Now, Patrick, your old man's got a hot horse runnin' here. One that's made him a bundle. I figure that money's drawn you here like a baby to mother's milk. So you go see your old man, Patrick. You tell him your sad story. I'm staying at the High Lonesome Lodge, room one twenty one. You bring me ten thousand in cash by tomorrow and I'll tear up your notes. You don't and I'll see to it that you're torn a new ass hole. You read me?"

15

The article was on the front page of the POST TIME, the national tabloid covering the world of horse racing. Under the dateline Sierra Vista Downs and under the heading "Call To The Post," the piece read:

Rebel, owned by Monty Bell of Midland, Texas, heads the field of ten hopefuls for Sunday's running of the 440 yard Oklahoma Quarter Horse Futurity to be held here in the shadows of the tall pines. This race, with its $750,000 purse, is the second jewel of the coveted Triple Crown.

Rebel, the odds-on-favorite, will face stiff competition from Halleluja, Sheik of Araby, Paragon of Merit, Right On, Bright Babe, Gray Badger, Mortgage Burner, Rags to Riches and Speedy Gonzales.

In the four trial heats for the upcoming race, Rebel, in the second division, posted the fastest time at :21.41; Bright Babe in the first division with :21.52; Gray Badger in the third division in the time of :21.55; and Halleluja in the fourth trial run was clocked at :21.60.

Paragon of Merit won the Texas Futurity, the first jewel in the Triple Crown, posting a time of :21.46 on a fast track. This powerful contender had trouble coming out of the gate during the trial run for the second jewel and finished half a length behind Gray Badger. Dock Trainham, Paragon of Merit's owner; J.P. Bates, trainer; and Sonny Rogers, wearing the silks will be pulling out all the stops to get their mount across the finish line ahead of the field to make it two out of three, a feat that has not been accomplished in the past five years. The Triple Crown here at Sierra Vista Downs has only been won by one horse since its inception twenty-two years ago.

The news story went on to detail the breeding of the contenders, their past performances and statistics on the trainers and jockeys representing the different stables.

The pervasive smell of loose money, the spoils, was ubiquitous around the track and the village. A seven hundred and fifty thousand dollar purse was to be waiting at the finish line of the tenth race on Sunday, the lion's share going to the winning horse. The pari-mutuel windows were set to pass out hundreds of thousands of dollars to bettors who, by shrewdness or blind luck, will have placed their bets on one or a combination of the win, place and show horses. Tout sheets and the Daily Racing Form were outselling Thursday's edition of the local newspaper ten to one. The Oklahoma Futurity was only one race of a four-day racing card but it was, like the Preakness during the Kentucky Derby, the second hurdle for the Triple Crown, and the featured race. Telephones in bookmakers' dens from Los Angeles to Atlantic City were busy computing the odds on the field and taking bets from people eager to lay down money on their selections.

The insistent ringing of the telephone brought Sonny out of the shower stall. Muttering expletives and wrapping a bath towel around his lean midriff, he tracked water from the bathroom, through the bedroom and across the small living room.

"Hello," he said sharply.

"Did I wake you?" asked an apologetic, blue-velvet voice from the other end of the line.

"No, I've been up quite a while. I was just getting out of the shower. What are you doing up this early, Cathy?"

"Oh, I'm sorry I rang you at a bad time but I wanted to catch you before you left for the track," she said. "I know you racing people go out early to exercise your horses while it's cool."

"You didn't catch me at a bad time," Sonny lied. "I was just fixin' to leave." He wondered how she had learned his telephone number. It was unlisted. But he did not want to ask a question that might embarrass her.

"I've tried several times to call you," Cathy said, "but I guess you spend most of your time at the track. I could never find you at home."

"Yeah," Sonny said. "About all I do here is change clothes and sleep. I tried to call you Tuesday but found out that you'd checked out. I figured you must have left town."

"Oh?" Cathy drawled the word out. "Well, I, uh, was away for a few days. I had to go home and pick up some more clothes," she quickened the pace and added a little laugh. "But I'm back now."

"Good," Sonny said. "Maybe we can get together again."

"I was hoping you'd suggest that. If you pin me down I'd probably have to confess that's why I forgot my manners and called you. Good girls don't do that," she added demurely.

"I saw you ride yesterday," Cathy continued. "I waved at you when you were in the winner's circle but you didn't see me. Too many pretty girls between us," she said over a little laugh.

"I wish I'd seen you," Sonny replied. "Knowin' you were in the stands would have made my day."

"I thought you had a pretty good day as it was," Cathy offered. "Won a race by four lengths and placed third on a maiden packing thirteen to one odds. Not bad for three mounts. And I see where you're standing second in the jockey ratings for this week. I was proud of you. Bragged to all my friends that I knew you."

"Are you going to the track today?" Sonny asked.

"I think so," Cathy replied.

"Got any special plans?"

"Nothing definite. Barbara said something about us going together. Why do you ask?"

"I've only got two mounts today," Sonny told her. "One in the second and one in the fifth. I'll be through early, and would like to join you in the stands, if that's OK."

"I'd love it," she replied with enthusiasm. I'll be in Box C5 in the Jockey Club."

A touch of irony edged Sonny's reply. "I may be a jockey but I'm not a member of the Jockey Club. That's a little rich for my blood."

"Oh," Cathy said. "Well, I'll tell you what. I'll leave a guest card for you at the gate. Will that be all right?"

"That's fine with me, if it's all right with you," Sonny said, detecting a slight rebuke over his cynical attitude. "I'll be there thirty minutes or so after the fifth."

"I'm going to hang a twenty dollar bill on the nose of each of your mounts," Cathy said, "and we'll split the winnings."

"I'll remember that when I'm in the stretch," Sonny laughed. "See you later." Singing a chorus of the old Hank Williams' song "Hey Good Looking," he headed back to the bathroom.

Sonny called her room on a house phone in the lobby. While he waited for her to come down, he thought about the afternoon at the track. He had been in his element, and he had enjoyed it. Barbara and Cathy drew him out and he found he enjoyed coaching them with their bets. They had all come out winners.

He saw her walking alone along the long hallway which led from the wing to the lobby. He had known horses that seemed to sense they were a cut above the average. Their bearing, their walk, their whole attitude showed self-confidence, maybe a touch of conceit. Cathy, her natural beauty highlighted by a golden tan, her stylish dress and her unaffected mannerism carried that same air of superiority. As she crossed the lobby, he had conflicting emotions. His instilled distrust of women and the usual inferiority complex that was part of him when he was away from the track and horses struggled against a budding sense of pride as he saw men turn their heads to admire Cathy. They rode the elevator to the mezzanine. The hostess in the Cattlemen's Club led them to a small table overlooking the lobby.

Dining on a six-ounce broiled tenderloin steak, Sonny began to relax. Cathy was easy to be with and she drew him out with her friendly manner and polite, but not intrusive questions. Sonny found himself wanting to tell her about himself, where he was from, how he found his way to the track and some stories about his racing career that he thought might amuse her. Over after-dinner coffee he even found himself talking about his hopes of becoming a trainer after he was too old to ride. It was later, when he thought back over their evening, that he realized their conversation had been mostly centered on him, that his few efforts to draw Cathy out had been politely, but deftly, sidetracked. She had maneuvered him into carrying the conversation.

After dinner Cathy suggested they go back to the lounge at the Inn. Holding her on the dimly lit dance floor, her perfumed, feminine body yielding to him, their thighs touching, her cheek lying softly against his as they moved in unison to the tune of a love song worked against Sonny's obsessions like gently waves caressing sand castles.

It was a little after midnight when they strolled, hand in hand, down the deserted hallway to stand in front of her room. Sonny released her hand and gently slid his arm around the small of her back. She yielded, turned to him, and moved into his encircling arms. She responded with a subtle willingness that quickly mounted to match Sonny's hard embrace and passionate kiss.

They clung to one another for a long moment, as the ground swell of aroused passions receded. Then he felt her loosen and start to move away. He dropped his arms slowly and she stepped back. They looked pensively at one another, their thoughts their own. Suddenly she leaned forward, kissed him on the lips with a hard but fleeting kiss. She stepped back and said: "It was a fun day, Sonny. I can't tell you when I enjoyed a day as much. Thank you. Will you call me?"

"It was fun," Sonny agreed. "I'll call you."

She reached into her handbag, took out the room key and handed it to him. He fumbled at fitting the key to the lock, with hands that were not as steady as when he held the reins on a charging horse. He finally managed to unlock the door and handed her the key. She reached up and touched him gently on the cheek. "Good night," she said softly. "Sweet dreams."

"Good night, Cathy." He watched as she stepped inside her room and slowly closed the door.

The radio in the pickup was playing one of Sonny's favorite songs, Linda Ronstadt singing "Blue Bayou." But he didn't hum or whistle along. He was absorbed with the inner conflict in his mind. A conflict between elation and caution.

16

Dock picked up the telephone

before it had completed its first ring. He was expecting J.P.'s call with the results of the day's racing card. There was that click again, like someone picking up an extension. It was the same little noise that he had been hearing when he would place a call. He studied and listened, but there was only the faint hum of the phone.

It was J.P.'s voice that broke the silence. "Dock, you there?"

"Yeah, I'm here," Dock replied. "Are you at a pay phone?"

"Yeah, the one by the corner of the barn."

"Give me that number. I'll call you back."

"Well, it's five, five, six, forty-two, seventy-three. You gonna call right back?"

"Yeah. You just wait there."

"Are you OK, Dock? Nothing wrong, is there?"

"No, and I'm all right," Dock replied hesitantly. "It's just that I, well, I've got an urgent call to the bathroom. I'll call you back in a few minutes," he said hurriedly.

Dock held the line open after J.P. hung up. There was a soft click, then the hum. He placed the receiver in its cradle, walked into the bathroom, waited a few minutes then flushed the commode. He walked softly across the room, let himself out the door then eased it shut behind him. He walked down the long hallway to the row of pay phones in the lobby. He deposited a quarter and dialed the number J.P. had given him.

No mention was made of Dock's rather unusual behavior, so he figured J.P. had accepted the bathroom story. After reporting on Paragon, J.P. told Dock that Sonny had ridden Shoemaker's Dandy to place in the second race, but drove in the field in the fifth.

"Sonny came in last on Gay Blade?" Dock questioned. "What happened? Last I knew that horse was figured for an easy win."

87

"That's right," J.P. replied. "He went in at three to two. He had trouble coming out of the gate. Tripped an' damned near went down."

"Damn!" Dock exclaimed. "Did Sonny get hurt?"

"No, but he sure could have. If they'd gone plumb down, Sonny would have been thrown right underneath the number five horse. But luckily, he was able to pick the horse up before it fell. After they got straightened out, Sonny laid the bat on an' they come aflyin'. But there was no way, in two furlongs, that he could catch up. I talked to Sonny after the race. He says he thinks the gate handler did something to throw the horse off balance just as the gate opened. Who knows?" J.P. said.

"Who was holdin' the horse's head?" Dock asked.

"Some fellow I don't know," J.P. replied.

"You reckon somebody got to him?" Dock asked.

"It happens," J.P. said.

"Who would you suspect, in this instance?" Dock asked.

"Well," J.P. responded. "Could have been any number of people. Maybe someone didn't want Gay Blade to win. The number eight horse, Handsome Jet, won and paid thirty-three dollars. Somebody could have had a bundle ridin' on it. Then again Dock, it could have been somebody wanting Gay Blade to either stumble or get bumped, and maybe go down; setting Sonny up for a nasty fall."

"That's the thought that bothers me," Dock said. "That's all we'd need is to have Sonny out of commission on Sunday. I've been concerned about that but didn't feel like I could ask him to lay off other mounts just for us. I sure as hell wouldn't feel very good with a new jockey on Paragon. I thing that'd be a helluva handicap, here at the last minute. I was relieved when you told me yesterday that you and Sonny had agreed he wouldn't ride after today so he'd be rested and ready for Sunday."

"Yeah, I agree," J.P. said. "A different jockey would be bad. Paragon knows Sonny. A stranger up would made a difference in his behavior. Anyway, Sonny was willing to lay off a day. And when you consider his cut of a futurity purse you can understand why he figures it's to his advantage, as well as ours.

"I'll canter Paragon on the track tomorrow morning," J.P. continued, "then on Sunday morning we can put him on the walker for a spell. That ought to do."

"I thing he's fine-tuned and ready, don't you?" Dock asked.

"He's fine as frog hair, Dock. If we get beat Sunday it will be because he's up against a better horse."

"Or," Dock injected, "somebody bushwhacks us. I'm coming out to the track. Meet me at the barn in a few minutes." He hung the receiver on the bracket and hurried across the lobby toward the front entrance.

Dock drove the mile and a half from the motel to the horseman's entrance to the track with his thoughts centered on what to say to J.P. The man had spent most of his life around the track. He was accustomed to the shady things that were considered by track people as part of the industry. Maybe I'm making mountains out of mole hills, Dock thought; suspecting someone's got my phone bugged. Maybe I've been watching too much television. But what about Sonny's close call today? "Damned if I know," he exclaimed.

J.P. was sitting on the tack box in front of Paragon's stall watching Robert, his new stable boy, load the manger with timothy.

"Let's go get a cup of coffee," Dock suggested. "Lock the doors to the stall and tell Robert to stay here and keep an eye on things. We won't be gone long."

"Wait until I grain Paragon before we go," J.P. said.

"Don't you trust the boy to do that?" Dock asked.

"I don't trust nobody but you or me to feed him grain. I know exactly how much I want fed and when I want it fed. You know how important that is. And I check what I feed to be sure it's clean. Some of this stuff we get has ergot in it, or maybe you'll find..."

"Yeah, or maybe," Dock interrupted. "If somebody could pick the lock on your grain box and plant a whiskey bottle, then they sure as hell could get in and doctor the grain with arsenic, couldn't they?"

The abrupt interruption and the possible implication of censure in Dock's statement caused J.P. to turn and look at his boss, a frown of concern crossing his ruddy features. "You tryin' to make a point?" he asked.

"Let's talk while we're walkin'," Dock said. As they made their way along the path towards the track and grandstand area, Dock continued: "J.P., what would you say if I said I think my phone at the motel is bugged?"

"Your phone's bugged?" J.P. questioned.

Dock explained his reasoning. He described the noise that sounded like an extension and the fact that he knew the room on the other side of the wall with his phone jack was occupied because he could hear the toilet flush. Yet he never heard voices or saw anyone come or go from that room.

"Well," J.P. drawled as he slowly nodded his head, "it all adds up."

"What adds up?" Dock asked.

"I hadn't said anything to you," J.P. replied, "because I didn't want to worry you until I was sure of something. But...," he paused, his brow wrinkled in concentration and his eyes squinted as he marshaled his thoughts.

"But what?" Dock prompted.

"Well," J.P. continued, "I've noticed a fellow hanging around our barn area the past few days. And he's damned sure not a horseman. He tries to dress like he belongs, but shit, it's obvious that he's as counterfeit in his get up as I would be in a three-piece business suit. Then, since we win the Texas, every time we've run Paragon against the stopwatch I've seen this same dude watchin' from back in the shadows of the grandstand. I figure he's holding a clock on us."

"I saw him the other day," Dock said. "You introduced him to me a couple of days ago. His name's Wayne something-or-other. I remember because he was from Midland and claimed to know Patrick."

"That's Wayne Belcheff, the gambler. He's also been watching Paragon's workouts. I figure he's probably watchin' all the futurity nominees, trying to figure how he's gonna lay his bets. Wayne likes the edge when he puts his money down. I read Wayne. It's the other fellow, the stranger, who concerns me. What the hell's his angle?"

"Hmmm," Dock puzzled.

"I'll tell you something else," J.P. added. "Tommy came over to see me the other night. I was already asleep on my cot in front of the stall door. I'm a light sleeper but he sure slipped up on me. I never even knew he was there until I heard someone whisper my name. I damned near jumped out of my bedroll. Remember, Tommy used to say he got along so well with Paragon because they're both black as sin? It was dark as the inside of a well digger's pocket an' I sure couldn't see anybody. By God, I'll admit I was boogered there for a few seconds until Tommy spoke again." J.P. chuckled. "Anyway, Tommy said he needed to tell me a few things. You see, Dock, when he left us to go to work for Scavarda I asked him to keep his eyes and ears open. To let me know if he picked up anything that might concern us or Paragon.

"You know, Dock, Tommy wouldn't talk to me out there on the walkway. He was worried someone might come along an' see us together talking and the word get back to Scavarda. 'Them people are tough, J.P.,' he said. Then he went on to say that he'd heard bits and pieces of talk around that bunch concerning what he said they called 'that black stud.'"

"What kind of talk?" Dock asked.

"Well, Tommy said he heard Scavarda and Yeager talking about Wall Street. Marvin was telling the old man about Wall Street's track record an' about how he traced back to Leo an' what a hot bloodline he had. Then one time when Tommy was cleaning a stall and they didn't know he was there, Marvin was telling Scavarda what Paragon's speed index was. Tommy said he knew Marvin had a fellow keepin' a stop watch on Paragon whenever we had him on the track."

"Like you say, J.P., it's beginning to come together," Dock said. "We'd better get back to the barn. We've been gone too long."

17

"How'd you get in here?"
Dock asked as he shut the door behind him.

"Easy. I told 'em at the desk that you were my old man. They gave me a key."

"How've you been?" Dock inquired as he moved to the center of the room to set his western-style panama on top of the bureau. He paused to stand for a few moments watching the evening news.

"OK, I guess," the young man replied from where he lounged in Dock's favorite recliner, the one he had brought from the ranch to make motel living a little more comfortable.

Dock glanced around the room, frowned, and walked over to sit in a straight-backed chair beside the table. The two men watched the wrap-up of the news without comment. At a break for a commercial, Dock turned his attention to the younger man and asked: "When did you get to town?"

"Couple of days ago," Patrick replied without taking his attention from the man on the television set who was hawking dog food.

Dock got up from his chair and walked into the bathroom. When he returned he was carrying a tumbler half full of amber fluid. "There's some whiskey in there if you want a drink," he said and indicated the bathroom with a thrust of his head.

"Got any beer?" Patrick asked.

"No."

After the national and local newscast had run, Dock suggested they go to the dining room for supper. After the meal, during which neither man said much beside the briefest amenities, they went back to the room. Dock unlocked the door for them and walked over to sit in the recliner. He took his boots off with the aid of a boot jack and slipped on a well-worn pair of bedroom slippers. Patrick turned the TV on and scanned the stations, finally settling on a rock music program.

"Turn it down some, that's too loud," Dock complained.

Patrick reduced the volume a half decibel then went over to stretch out on the bed. "I hear Paragon won a big race last week," he commented.

"If you're gonna lie on the bed, take off those dirty boots," Dock directed.

"Hell, it's only a motel room," Patrick argued.

"That doesn't make any difference," Dock reprimanded. "Right now it's my home. That's a nice spread and your boots are dirty. Take 'em off, or get off the bed."

Patrick sat up, pulled off the worn boots and dropped them on the floor. He lay back down, laced his arms beneath his head and said: "Paragon's that black horse colt out of that ole mare you bought in Amarillo a couple of years ago, isn't he?"

"Yep," Dock replied.

"That was the mare an' her colt that mom spent so much time with," Patrick said. "I remember that she practically raised the colt on a bottle 'cause the mare wasn't giving any milk. Colt woulda probably died if it hadn't been for mom."

"Well," Dock said, "the old mare was in pretty bad shape and your mother certainly had a hand in the colt's survival. That's the kind of woman she was."

"How much money did we win?" Patrick asked.

Dock caught Patrick's use of the plural pronoun. He looked at the young man who was apparently engrossed watching the gyrating antics of the rock musicians on the TV screen. Finally Dock replied: "Well, it was a good purse."

"Dock," Patrick said, still watching the television. "I'm in a little bind, temporarily, and I need some money."

Always the same, Dock thought. Always needing to be bailed out of one jam after another. Will he ever be worth a damn? Dock looked at his adopted son: worn clothes that needed washing, scraggly hair that hung down to his shoulders and a mustache that needed trimming. Certainly no pride or self-respect in evidence. Dock thought of Martha. He thought about her fastidious ways, about her hopes and aspirations, her abiding love for her boy from infancy through the trying teenage years, and to the very day of her passing.

Raising Patrick had been the only serious point of contention in their marriage. Dock believed that Martha spoiled the boy. He reasoned that she carried a guilt complex for her part in a broken home and the separation of the boy from his father, and she did not want the problems of disciplining a spoiled son, her son, to be disruptive to Dock's set way of life or a threat to their marriage. Whenever problems with the boy had arisen Dock had forced himself to remember the promises he had made to Martha and the responsibility he had assumed when he adopted the baby boy. In retrospect, he had to admit he had not lived up to his vows of parenthood. Dock had been a bachelor before his marriage to Martha. He soon came to realize that Partick, in his formative years, needed a man's image and influence, as well as discipline, for guidance. Dock was sure that Martha also saw this need but she seemed to resent Dock's early attempts at disciplining or offering guidance to the boy. The only serious threat to their marriage was years ago when they quarreled heatedly over Dock losing his temper when he caught Patrick sassing his mother. Dock had grabbed the boy up, laid him across his knees and spanked him.After that run in, Dock bridled himself. He stood aside and left Patrick's upbringing to Martha.

Hell, Dock thought as he looked at the young man lying there on the bed, he wasn't a bad kid, just spoiled. If he's a maverick now, it was because Martha and he had failed in their parental responsibilities. Martha for being too lenient and protective in the formation years and too reluctant to admit her mistakes and powerless to rectify them in the later years. Dock recognized his shortcoming as side-stepping the issue, taking the path of least resistance. Both Martha and I put the well-being of our marriage, our surface happiness, ahead of our charge of shaping the boy's character, he reflected.

Dock thought about the matter as he watched Patrick, who was seemingly without a care beyond keeping time with the music. If we'd faced up to it, Dock thought with chagrin and guilt, halter broke the boy, taught him to lead and to accept discipline, tempering our actions with love instead of letting him run loose and wild, he'd no doubt be a much better man today.

"What kind of a bind are you in this time?" Dock asked.

"My unemployment's run out," Patrick replied. "I need some living money till I can go back to work. They told me over in Odessa that the drilling rigs ought to start up again pretty soon."

"Who told you? The boys in the pool hall?" Dock snorted.

"That's just what the talk is," Patrick replied.

"Patrick, you're either gullible as a turkey or you think I'm stupid. There isn't going to be any drilling of any consequence until crude gets above twenty dollars. There'll damned sure be no work for you in the oil patch with crude bringing twelve to fourteen, like it is now. Why don't you go home? You could give Mario a hand."

"Man, I need to make some money. I don't need to be wastin' my time helping some wet-back build fence," Patrick grumbled.

"I'll pay you wages," Dock replied evenly. "That would at least get you by until something else turns up."

"Shit, man, I'm talkin' about money. I can't make it on cowboy wages," Patrick snapped, and then in a more appeasing tone added: "Anyway, a driller or tool pusher sure as hell isn't gonna come hunting me on the ranch to offer me a job. That's why I need to be in town."

"Patrick, the drilling rigs are going to stay stacked for as long as the majors can import crude for twenty dollars or less. They can't develop a producing well and pay for it with that kind of market. And there's no telling how long this situation will last. Those camel herders are sittin' on an ocean of oil. I'll bet they can produce a barrel of crude for two or three bucks. You might as well face up to it and get lined out in some other direction."

"I don't know anything but oil field work," Patrick argued.

"I've offered to send you to school, but you didn't want to go," Dock reminded Patrick, with a strained tolerance edging his words. "You turned down college. So how about going to one of those vocational schools? You've always like to mess with motors and machinery. You could learn to be a mechanic. They make good money."

Patrick turned his attention from the TV screen to look at Dock. After a few moments he sat up, put his feet over the edge of the bed and said: "I don't have the kind of money it would take to go to school."

"I'd pay your way. You know that," Dock said.

"What do you think it would cost?" Patrick asked.

"Oh, I don't know," Dock replied. "It doesn't make any difference what it costs. I'll see you through, if you'll promise to apply yourself and learn something."

"I'd have to have living expenses, tuition, books, some clothes and all that crap," Patrick said. "It'd run into a lot of money. It'd cost more than you think."

"I said I didn't care what it costs," Dock responded, encouraged by the possibility of a solution to the problem. "My only restriction would be that you'd have to make a hand. When you fail to make your grades, or whatever they do in a vocational school, it would be back to the ranch for you, no argument."

"I'll tell you what, dad," Patrick said as he leaned forward and looked hard at his stepfather. "Going to school for a couple of years like you're talking would cost you at least ten grand, and that's just what I need to get me by until I find a job. You're offering to pay for the schooling. All I'm asking is that you loan me that money. And I'll pay you back. Deal?"

95

"Ten thousand!" Dock exclaimed. "I thought you said you just needed money to pay some living expenses."

Both men sat, Patrick waiting for Dock's anger to subside, and Dock wanting his heart palpitations to ease and his hands to relax their death grip on the arms of the chair. After a few minutes Dock said: "Ten thousand dollars. You planning to live pretty high on the hog, aren't you?"

"Well, you gotta figure that I owe a few debts around," Patrick replied.

The encouraging thought that Patrick might continue his schooling faded like a dream. Feelings of stupidity and chagrin engulfed Dock as he realized how easily he had been duped. The secondary reaction, that of total defeat and frustration, was eclipsed by smoldering, rising anger. He sat there, dead in the water, speechless, saddled with a problem he could not fully comprehend, and for which he had no solution.

Ten thousand dollars. These young people who've grown up during the oil boom have no idea of the value of a dollar, Dock thought. But the money isn't the main issue. How many times have I bailed this boy out of one jam or another? Where does it stop? When does he grow up and accept the responsibilities of being a man? One thing's for sure: he'll never stand on his own two feet as long as I keep propping him up. We should've broken his plate, weaned him years ago. Helping him has been like pouring water down a prairie dog hole. There's no end to it. I've been pissin' against the wind.

He dropped his eyes to stare unseeing at the brown rug between his feet. He pursed his lips and slowly shook his head in a gesture of futility. He felt his shoulders sag under the weight of the responsibility. He heaved a heavy sigh, looked up at Patrick and said: "Patrick, I'm not going to give you ten thousand dollars. You bring me a list of what bills you owe. I'll look at 'em and I'll probably end up paying anything that's reasonable and legitimate. Then I'll give you a couple hundred bucks, enough for you to get a hair cut and some clean clothes. Then you go home and stay there until after the racing season is over. When I get home we'll talk about your future."

"Bull shit!" Patrick stormed as he jumped to his feet. "You're tryin' to treat me like I'm some fuckin' kid! Sendin' me to go sit in the corner till you're ready to talk to me about my future," he mimicked in a mincing tone. "No way, man. I want to tell you something, dad! One of the girls at the bank told me that you've been dipping into my mother's estate. You've borrowed a chunk of money from it. And I also know that the banker took a mortgage on the ranch for the estate to secure those loans.

"Yeah, you adopted me, but shit, mom probably made you do that before she'd let you crawl in her bed. You've never liked me an' I know damned well I won't get a shittin' thin dime from you. But I'm here to tell you that I'm the beneficiary of mom's estate, so, by God, I hold a mortgage on the ranch. You can either give me what I want now or I'll get a lawyer an' claim my inheritance."

18

The ringing of the phone caught Dock by surprise. It was just a little after five and he was shaving. J.P.'s routine morning report came at five thirty, and he was punctual. He's early, Dock thought as he shut off his shaver and headed for the telephone. Apprehension began to build as he left the bathroom and walked around the bed to approach the ringing telephone on the bedside table. Possible explanations for the untimely call raced through his mind. Was something wrong at the track? A problem with Paragon? You don't suppose J.P.'s drunk again? Maybe it's Mario calling from the ranch. It was with dread and a knot building in the pit of his stomach as he reached to pick up the receiver of the jangling phone. "Hello?" he queried.

"Good morning, Mister Trainham, I hope I didn't call too early. I was afraid you might get off to the track and I would miss you."

Uncertainty as to who was on the other end of the line replaced the dread of a moment ago. It wasn't J.P. or Mario. "Who'm I talking to?" Dock asked.

"Marvin Yeager, Mister Scavarda's trainer."

"Oh, yes, Marvin, what can I do for you?"

"Mister Trainham, Mister Scavarda would like to have you join him for breakfast this morning."

"Here at the motel?" Dock asked.

"No sir, at Mister Scavarda's home in Ponderosa Canyon."

"Well, I guess I could do that," Dock replied. His mind probing for probably reasons and the implications of this unexpected meeting with a man he considered an adversary, even though he'd never met him.

"I'll arrange to have you picked up there at your motel whenever you're ready," Yeager said.

"Well," Dock said, "I'll have to wait here until after I get a call from the track. That'll be at five thirty. How about six?"

"That'll be fine. There'll be a taxi waiting for you in front of the motel at six."

"A taxi? Who all's going to be there?" Dock asked.

"There'll just be you, me and Mister Scavarda. The boss thinks it's best to have a taxi pick you up. You know how the word would get around and rumors go to flying if somebody saw you getting in my pickup and driving off with me."

"Well," Dock drawled, "you can send a taxi. It can show me the way, but I'll drive my pickup. That way I'll have my own transportation when I'm ready to leave."

"All right, sir. The taxi will be in front of the motel at six."

Dock's second call came on schedule. J.P. reported that everything was fine. Paragon had a good night and was eating good.

"Looks like it's going to be a pretty day, Dock," J.P. commented.

"Yeah," Dock replied. "Say, you haven't seen or heard anything about that Scavarda fellow or his crew, have you?"

"No."

"You haven't talked to Tommy lately?"

"Not since that night he came and woke me up," J.P. replied. "Why, something up?"

"I had a call this morning from Marvin Yeager. Scavarda wants to meet with me over breakfast. I didn't ask why an' Yeager didn't volunteer anything. But you can bet your bottom dollar it isn't just to break bread together."

"No tellin' what they've got on their minds," J.P. said, his voice betraying concern. "You want me to go with you? Kinda even up the odds?"

"No, but I want you to stay there at the barn. Don't leave. Send Robert to get you anything you need. I'll be there as soon a I can."

"Don't worry about me. You thinkin' maybe we got a problem?"

"I'm damned if I know what they're up to, J.P.; I'd guess that Scavarda's not given up on trying to get me to sell. What do you think?"

"Well, I don't know, Dock. In this business there's no telling what they might have on their minds, especially when we're dealin' with somebody like Scavarda. There's stories floatin' around the backside about him an' his bunch. From what I've heard they're tough, an' they're heavy-handed when it comes to handlin' horses or people."

"You've never mentioned hearing anything about 'em."

"Well, I know you don't take much stock in backside gossip," J.P. responded, "and anyway, I didn't want to add to your worries."

"What have you heard?" Dock asked.

"Well, just that they're not in this business for fun and games. You remember three weeks ago when they booted in a long shot? It was in the seventh race on Saturday."

"That was that gray, leggy horse with the Rodriquez kid up, wasn't it?" Dock asked.

"Yeah, that was the one," J.P. confirmed. "Well, people in the know say the horse was hyped-up. The track vet gathered samples of urine and saliva to run a test, like they always do on the first place horse. But somewhere between taking the samples and getting them to the lab there musta been a switcharoo. The horse tested negative, or least the samples the lab received did."

"Well," Dock drawled, "I don't think they're the only ones pulling that kind of crap."

"That's for sure," J.P. agreed. "Then you remember a couple months ago when Jack Roberts, that gate handler, was busted for dealin' drugs?"

"Yeah," Dock replied. "That was the fellow you said you were surprised about. You figured he wasn't for sale."

"That's him. And I still think he's a straight shooter. The word is he wouldn't take a payoff from one of Scavarda's boys to jimmy a horse at the gate. The horse he was holding ended up beatin' Scavarda's horse. About a week or so after the race the narc boys got an anonymous tip. They found a stash of coke in a dummy spare tire on Jack's pickup. I think he was set up for the fall. You might say a little lesson for the rest of the backside bunch."

There was silence while Dock let the implication of J.P.'s story sink in. He cleared his throat and said: "Well, I guess I better be going."

"Be careful, Dock," J.P. admonished. "Don't let 'em box you in."

"I'll see you at the barn in a little while," Dock replied and hung up the phone.

One of the local churches was piping devotional music over a public address system as Dock walked out onto the motel parking lot and into the freshness of a high country, autumn morning. The sounds of the organ music lifting over the village and the sun shining in a clear blue sky seemed incongruous to Dock whose mind was bothered with the thoughts of drugged horses and the power of manipulating money.

The taxi, with its motor idling, was parked in front of the lobby entrance in the area reserved for guest to load and unload their baggage. The driver was slumped in his seat, concentrating on a racing schedule. Dock walked across the paved lot to his pickup, unlocked the door, climbed in, started the motor, backed out and drove up behind the waiting taxi and honked his horn. The driver glanced at his rear view mirror, sat up, laid the racing form on the dash and eased the yellow cab off onto the frontage road. They headed southwest, through the business section and up a winding canyon into a residential area.

It was always a wonder to Dock, the number and the locations of the dwellings set among the steep-sided mountains and shadowy canyons. The owners, who came to their summer homes from Texas, called them "cabins," even though they might have cost a quarter of a million dollars to build. Except for the business buildings along the two main streets of the village there was no semblance of planning or order. Houses were scattered among the towering evergreens, some on the rocky crests like the aeries of an eagle, some nestled on level plots among the pines on the mountainsides, and some, defying floods, on the canyon bottoms. Most of the dwellings were mountain-type homes, some rustic cabins, some very impressive with address signs like the one Dock saw that proclaimed: "The Byrds of San Antonio Roost Here."

The cab driver was a man possessing great talent in his line of work and Dock had to drive with intent to keep the battered taxi in sight on the winding road that branched into side canyons. They turned off the canyon blacktop and onto a graveled road that led up a smaller canyon. Around a bend the way was blocked by a wrought iron gate flanked by high rock walls that tied into the steep canyon slopes. The taxi slowed and made a half circle in front of the gate. As Dock pulled up and slowed to a stop the cab driver honked his horn, waved, and headed back the way he had come. The iron gates parted and swung slowly open. Dock drove through and eased his pickup along a driveway that circled a beautifully landscaped rock garden and fronted a large expensive home built of quarried sandstone. The architecture spoke of the owner's desire to be a part of the rustic mountainous community, but certainly in an ostentatious way. Marvin Yeager was standing on the front deck holding a coffee cup.

"Get down, Mister Trainham," he greeted in the old countrified salutation that dated back to the days when people travelled on horseback or in buggies.

Dock stepped out of his pickup and walked across the gravel drive and up the four red flagstone steps to the porch.

Yeager extended his hand. "Good morning, sir. Could I interest you in a cup of coffee?"

"You could," Dock replied as they exchanged firm handshakes.

Yeager led the way over to a table that held a silver service and coffee mugs. "Cream or sugar?" he asked as he poured.

"Black," Dock answered.

The horse trainer handed Dock a cup, the coffee steaming in the early morning coolness. "Sit down," he invited, indicating a row of porch chairs.

Yeager saw the questioning look that clouded Dock's features as they moved towards the porch chairs. "Mister Scavarda will be out in a few minutes," he said rather sheepishly.

Dock frowned in aggravation. "I planned to be at the track by seven-thirty," he said.

"Mister Scavarda is not an early riser," Yeager apologized, "but we knew that you'd want to get out to the track early. The cook told me Mister Scavarda is up, so I'm sure he'll be along in a few minutes."

During the trip from the motel Dock had mulled over the happenings that had occurred since his first meeting with Yeager. Not just circumstantial, Dock knew, but pressure tactics that he laid at Scavarda's door. Like Tommy going to work for Scavarda, the planted whiskey bottle in the feed bin, and the suspicion that they were listening to his phone calls. By the time he had arrived at the Scavarda home he was not in a congenial frame of mind. Now, to compound it, he felt that it was a personal affront when the man who had called for a meeting, at the time and place of his choosing, was late. The son-of-a-bitch is showing me my place, Dock thought as he took a seat. Bringing me up here to a meeting on his turf and then letting me cool my heels, waiting until he's good and ready to see me.

"I guess your horse is ready for the big event tomorrow?" Yeager said in a manner and tone that implied small talk, not intended to be a breach of propriety between competitors.

"Ready as he'll ever be," Dock retorted. He glanced at the man sitting beside him. Don't blame him, he told himself. He just works for the bastard. He knows it's a damned insult for his boss to be late an' keep me waitin'. He's as nervous over the situation as I am agitated.

"Let me warm your coffee," Yeager offered. He got up and brought the coffee pot over to refill their cups.

Dock looked at his watch: Six-twenty, and it would take fifteen or twenty minutes to drive from here to the track. He leaned back against his chair, crossed his right leg over the left, and thought: I'll give the son-of-a-bitch five more minutes then he can go to hell, 'cause I'm leaving.

It was several moments later when the front door opened. Dock turned his head to look at the man approaching. His first impression was of power.

He's built like a damned Jersey bull, he thought. Barrel-chested and short-legged. I'd hate to have him get me in a bear hug.

Yeager got up and poured coffee for his boss who took the cup without comment. "Mister Trainham, this is Mister Scavarda," Yeager said.

Dock stood up and extended his right hand. The two men, one in a western-cut white shirt, saddleman's Levi trousers and scuffed cowboy boots; the other in a white Bill Blass sport shirt, blue serge trousers and bare feet encased in well-worn bedroom slippers. The two exchanged firm handshakes and made their pointed appraisals.

"Sit down, Mister Trainham," Scavarda indicated the chair that Dock had just vacated. "Marvin, go tell the cook to come take Mister Trainham's breakfast order." Yeager started for the front door. "Warm the man's coffee before you go," Scavarda instructed his horse trainer.

The horseman stopped, turned to the table, unplugged the coffee pot and stepped over to top off the cup that Dock held out to him.

The two men, left alone, sat nursing their coffee, seeming absorbed by the view of the landscaped, well tended yard and the peaceful, forested slope that extended beyond.

"Nice place you got here," Dock commented.

"I just lease the place," Scavarda said. "Belongs to a Texan. He built it, an' was gonna pay for it with oil money. He used to fly over here in his Lear jet. Now he can't afford the gasoline to drive over, so he leases it to me an' I pay for it with money I get for shippin' in oil with my tanker fleet from Saudi Arabia." Scavarda laughed at the irony. "I'll say one thing for the poor bastard: he knew how to live. This place isn't as big as a place I got in the Catskills, but it's comfortable. The man went first class."

"Thirty dollar crude built a lot of those pipe dreams," Dock said. "Some people seem to forget that what goes up will likely come down. I'm not an oilman myself but I've noticed over the years that it's a business that has a history of highs and lows, like everything else."

"Everything but taxes," Scavarda growled. "Taxes just go up. I've got an office full of high-price paper shufflers trying to figure out how I can keep some of the money I got coming in. That's what's got me sittin' here talking to you now. They told me this horse business was a good investment for a write-off. You know what I mean, don't you Trainham?"

Dock looked out over the yard and stifled the urge to comment on a subject that vexed him: Cattlemen, like himself, were at a disadvantage competing with people who were in the business as a side line. People who sold their cattle on the same market Doc did, yet could offset losses against taxable income from some other business. People like this Scavarda, Doc thought. If I were to sell Paragon to him, he'd use it as a write-off against the big money he's making bringing in foreign oil. And I'd have to pay capital gain. That doesn't wash.

If his host was aware that Dock had evaded the question, he gave no sign. He's just talking to hear himself talk, Dock thought. He's not interested in any comment I'd have to make.

The front door opened and Yeager came out followed by a man in a chef's outfit. "Luigi, fix this man what he wants for breakfast," Scavarda instructed and indicated Dock with a thrust of his chin.

"What's your pleasure, sir?" the cook asked.

"Bacon and eggs and a little orange juice, if you've got it." Dock replied.

"How you like you eggs?"

"Scrambled dry with a little salsa picante, if you have any."

The cook hefted the coffee pot to check the contents. "Coffee?" he asked, and looked first at his boss and then at Dock. Scavarda held out his cup, and Dock said: "Mine's fine, thanks."

Dock watched with some amusement as the cook filled Scavarda's cup, look right past Yeager, a fellow employee, set the coffee pot down and returned to the house. Yeager stepped over to refill his own cup. Independent as a cow camp cook, Dock thought and chuckled to himself at the contrary, independent behavior of cooks in general.

The telephone on the porch table rang. Yeager stepped over to answer it and after the salutation, listened for a moment then said: "Mister Scavarda, you're wanted on the phone. Do you want to take in here or in your office?"

"I'll take it here," Scavarda replied. "Who is it?"

"Said his name's Wayne Belcheff," Yeager answered.

"I don't know anybody by that name," Scavarda grumbled as he rose to go to the phone on the serving table. "Excuse me Trainham," he said as he picked up the receiver. "Hello," he barked, "this is Vince Scavarda."

Dock thought about the name of the caller while Scavarda was occupied with the call. Then it dawned on him and he thought: hell, that's the fellow J.P. introduced me to the other day. The gambler from Midland who said he knew Patrick.

"First thing," Scavarda spoke into the telephone receiver, his voice edged with displeasure, "I want to know how the hell you got hold of my unlisted phone number." There was silence on the porch as Scavarda listened to the explanation. Then Scavarda said, "I might be interested. I'll have Manny, an associate of mine, come talk to you. Where are you staying?" Scavarda listened to the reply then said, "Manny'll be at your motel in an hour." He placed the receiver back in its cradle, went back to his seat and sat down. "Trainham," he said as he turned his attention to Dock, "Marvin tells me you've turned down my offer to buy your horse." It was a statement, but those probing, dark eyes asked why, and the shadow of a frown showed annoyance.

Dock found himself feeling like a school boy being confronted by the principal over an infraction of the rules. Then anger rose, both against the inquisitor and against himself for letting the man's bullheaded arrogance intimidate him. Bridling his rising emotions, he replied: "that's right Scavarda, Paragon's not for sale."

"I offered you eighty grand. You think your horse is worth more?"

This isn't going to be a simple matter of just saying no, and having it accepted, Dock thought. This is a stubborn man. He's use to having his way and I don't know how to answer his question. There's a reasonable value to the horse, but if I set a price, something that wouldn't make me out a complete fool, this fellow might just take me up on it. He may be that bullheaded.

"Scavarda, I haven't put a price on the horse. I told Yeager when he came to see me the other day that the horse is just not for sale."

"Trainham, Yeager tells me you're a cattle rancher. So, you're a businessman. You buy and sell cattle, don't you? You know the world turns on trading. Everything, everybody, big or little, has a value, a price. It's just a matter here of you settin' a price on your nag and me deciding if I want to pay your price. We're both busy men. We don't have time to play games."

A maid was holding open the front door, waiting so as not to interrupt her employer. When there was a pause, the young lady said quietly: "Breakfast is served."

The three men rose from their chairs and walked single file, Scavarda in the lead andYeager trailing behind Dock, along the porch. They entered through heavy, hand-sculptured, double doors into a large, ranch-style living room. Dock glanced around, impressed by the furnishings and the architecture. Most of the eastern wall was faced with a veneer of mortared flagstone from ceiling to hardwood floor and encased an outsized, wood-burning fireplace fronted by a half-circle, sandstone hearth. Mounted over the fireplace was a bull elk head, a seven-by-seven trophy, Dock noted. A sumptuous, matched set of magenta-colored leather upholstered couch and easy chairs bracketed a large Hereford steer hide that covered the floor in front of the hearth. Big, colorfully-patterned Navajo rugs covered other sections of the gleaming oak flooring. Western-scene paintings and mounted game heads, among which was an antelope which Dock appraised as probably qualifying for a listing in Boone and Crocket, hung on knotty pine, tongue-and-groove walls. A unique chandelier fashioned from deer horns was suspended from the ceiling.

Scavarda led them to an alcove at the north corner of the living room which served as a breakfast area. The Mexican serving woman stood beside double swinging doors which led into the kitchen. Scavarda took his place at the head of the linen-covered table. "Sit here, Trainham," he directed Dock, and indicated the place at his right. Yeager took the seat to the left of his boss.

They ate without small talk, the serving girl seeing to their needs. Scavarda commented about tasteless food and the ancestry of the doctor who had put him on a salt-free-diet. After the meal he directed that they adjourned to the front porch.

Dock was beginning to feel nervous tension tighten the muscles in the back of his neck. He was anxious to get to the track. "I have no intention of putting a price on Paragon and I wish to hell Scavarda would accept that fact and bring this waste of time to an end," he said to himself.

Scavarda offered Dock a cigar, which he declined. "These are special-made, handrolled the old way," Scavarda coaxed as he took a pen knife from his trouser pocket and cut off the end of the cigar. He passed the rolled, dark tobacco leaves over his tongue, took out a lighter, flicked a flame and lit the cigar, emitting a cloud of gray, pungent smoke. He leaned back, inhaled slowly through the cigar to savor the flavor, then slowly exhaled the bluish gray smoke. "That's a damned fine cigar," he said as he held it out to admire it. "Ought to be. A box of 'em costs me over sixty bucks. You don't know what you're missin', Trainham."

Dock did not reply as he fought back the almost overpowering urge to get up from the chair and thank the man for the breakfast and be on his way. But he sat without comment, crossing and uncrossing his legs and fidgeting while Scavarda went through the painstaking, unhurried process of savoring his cigar, seemingly oblivious to anything or anybody else.

"Trainham," Scavarda finally said, "I started working on the docks, handling cargo, when I was fourteen years old. I took my lumps. I worked my ass off an' kept my mouth shut. I saw that a man could spend his miserable life working with his back and the muscles in his arms, an' leave this world with damned little more than he had when he came into it. Or he could use his head an' be a boss.

"I used my head, Trainham, I saved enough money to buy me a suit, a white shirt an' a tie. I let the chumps handle the freight. I handled their deals with the people who owned the freight. Now I have my own fleet of ships. I'm the boss. I pay people to do the work. I pay Yeager a damned good salary to look after my horses. I got enough sense to know I'm no horseman so I listen to him when he tells me I ought to have your horse in my stable. I made you a good offer but you turned me down. Yeah, your horse won a Futurity. You know as well as I do that might have been a flash-in-the-pan. You may end up selling him in a claiming race for a couple a grand, or maybe it'll break a leg an' you'll have to eat the son-of-a-bitch. Who knows. It's all a big gamble, Trainham, an' I'm offering to let you walk away a big winner while I take the gamble."

Dock started to reply, but Scavarda went on. "We make our deal here and now. Like Yeager told you, I'll pay you however you want: cash now, part payment now and the rest later, however it suits your tax picture. You go ahead and run the fuckin' horse in the Futurity tomorrow. If he lucks out and runs in the money, half the purse is yours. If the son-of-a-bitch falls and breaks a leg, he's mine. Trainham, you've never had a better offer. We agree now an' I'll have the papers drawn up and ready for you to sign before lunch."

Am I supposed to have a choice in this matter? Dock thought. Doesn't seem like it, and the bastard is about half convincing.

"What do you say, Trainham? We got a deal?" Scavarda pressed.

Maybe it was Dock's independence, his dislike for being bulldozed around. Maybe it was the ever-present memories of Martha and her horse, the recollections of their time together raising the colt during Martha's last days and the resulting alleviation that was a balm against the sorrow and the agony. Maybe it was J.P. and his dependency on the horse in his struggle to overcome his drinking problem, regain his self-confidence and win back his family. Maybe it had to do with wanting to play out the hand that chance had dealt him.

"I appreciate your offer, but I guess I'll let it pass. "Dock said slowly.

A flush darkened Scavarda's swarthy face. His jaw muscles bunched as he bit down on the cigar. His eyes narrowed and his heavy brows knitted. "You baitin' me, Trainham?" he asked, anger edging his words. "All right. Goddamnit, I'll give you a hundred grand! Not a goddamn cent more!"

"Scavarda, the horse isn't for sale," Dock retorted, his eyes snapping in anger.

Scavarda rose from his chair. He took the cigar from his mouth and threw it over the porch railing onto the manicured lawn. He turned to glower at

Dock, who was rising to leave. "You wanna play games, heh? Goddamnit, cowboy, I'll show you how Vince Scavarda plays games!" He turned on his heel and stomped across the porch and into the house.

As Dock walked past the front door on his way off the porch, he heard Scavarda's voice coming from inside the house.

"Manny! Come here. I got a job for you," the voice said.

19

The groan registered a mixture of pain and gratification as Sonny yielded to the ministrations of Simon's powerful hands and kneading fingers. The near fall yesterday had wrenched his back, and his sudden, almost involuntary reaction to the horse stumbling had left his shoulders and neck muscles stiff and sore.

Simon was a fixture around the horse barns of the New Mexico and Texas tracks. His occupation was as a masseur and para-chiropractor working in the jockeys' locker rooms. He supplemented this income by sorting and weighing the rumors that floated around the backside and placing his bets accordingly. He carried more money away from the pari-mutuel windows than he left there. A thick head of graying, kinky hair and a muscular body that was softening gave evidence that he was in the early winter of his life. His unusual height was a probable expression of Zulu ancestry.

Simon was a very solitary person. Sonny, because of his mature and reserved demeanor, was one of the few people he allowed to get close to him. He stoically accepted his station in the world of the Caucasian, not in a subservient manner but as a reaction to an unalterable fact of life. Possibly in retaliation, he had his own caste system. The black and the brown skinned hirelings who mucked out the stables and washed the horses were, to Simon, nonentities. He ignored them, as he did the horsey, white gentry.

On those selected days, generally a Thursday, when the jockeys pooled their money to bet on a horse carrying long odds, it was Simon who would show up at the pari-mutuel window just before the closing bell sounded to place a large wager. And it was Simon who, more often than not, stood at the pay window to collect the winnings after a jockey booted the long shot to lead the field across the wire.

Simon gave Sonny's shoulder and neck muscles a final kneading, slapped him on the back and said: "Go take a hot shower, man, an' I think you'll be ready to go steppin' with that classy filly I hear you're running with."

"Who told you that?" Sonny asked as he sat up on the massage table.

"Rodriquez told me he lined you up with a blind date, a girl that runs with his chick," Simon answered.

"Well," Sonny said, "he did talk me into a blind date. Considering who he is, it was against my better judgement, but it turned out all right. I don't know how Rodriquez got involved with these girls. They're class, that's for sure, not like the track-tramps he generally runs with."

"More power to you man," Simon said as he wiped his hands on a towel. "A man needs a woman, some men need one at their side all the time, an' some just occasionally. Myself, I'm the occasional type. But my needs now is more than a wham, bam, thank you ma'am." Simon walked over to put the bottles of liniment and rubbing alcohol in a locker while Sonny slipped on the top of his sweat suit.

"There was a time in my youth, when the object of courtin' a woman was to get her between the sheets," Simon continued. "But now, I find my needs go deeper than the flesh. Don't be jumpin' to no conclusions Sonny. There may be frost on the roof and the fires of desire have died down some, but there's still live coals in the box. But now laying a woman just for the carnal pleasure of sex, without the givin' an' receivin' of love and affection, doesn't satisfy the needs of my soul, and at my age, the needs of the soul are more important that the needs of the flesh. You understand what I'm sayin'?"

"I guess so," Sonny replied seriously. "I've never been much of a hand with the girls. Oh, I've chased some, got kinda serious a time or two, but you know what hangs around the tracks. Most of 'em are either kids looking at the glamour, prick-teasers playing a fellow along for an inside tip, or hookers tryin' to turn a trick. I've found that I'm better off paying attention to my horses. Anyway, Simon, I couldn't make out in a whore house if I was wearin' a brace of six guns an' packin' a sack of gold." The two men laughed as Sonny headed for the shower room.

"Play it cool, Sonny. You have a real comer in that black stud. Lots of people are talking' about the chances for you an' that horse in tomorrow's race. Smell the roses, Sonny, but watch out for the thorns," Simon called after his friend.

"I've been around some, Simon. Don't worry. I always untrack a strange horse before I mount, and ease it around under a tight rein before I give it its head. That can sure keep a man out of a lot of trouble, you know," Sonny replied over his shoulder.

It was Cathy's suggestion, something that would never have occurred to Sonny, to be away from the track and miss a Saturday card. But the more he thought about it the more it appealed to him. Cathy was going to have the hotel pack a picnic lunch and they were going to drive up into the mountains for the afternoon.

"So you've found yourself a girl friend," J.P. commented after Sonny told him why he would not be at the track. "I'd about decided you didn't know why God created Eve. You go an' have a good time," the veteran trainer said as he put his arm across the shoulders of his friend and jockey. "Gettin' away from the track for a spell will be good for you. You'll be ready an' rarin' to go tomorrow."

"It might be a welcome change to be around somebody beside you ignorant horsemen, somebody who smells of perfume and not horse shit. But do you reckon you all can run twelve races without screwin' up if I'm not here to supervise?" Sonny quipped.

"Well, we'll sure do our level best," J.P. replied in all seriousness, "but no doubt, the stewards will screw things up without you here to keep 'em straight. Say, do I know this girl you're datin'? I might ought to check her out, you know. Give my approval."

"I doubt if you know her an' I'll just have to take my chances without your approval," Sonny bantered. "Seriously, J.P., her name's Catherine. She doesn't hang around the track much. She's got a membership in the Jockey Club, but I doubt if she's ever been down here to the backside. The few friends of hers that I've met sure don't smell of horse liniment."

"Sounds like you're runnin' with the papered gentry," J.P. said.

"I'll admit that I'm damned sure out of my class," Sonny replied, "and I catch myself wondering what I'm doing there."

"I ran with some of the registered fillies when I was a young buck playing polo," J.P. said thoughtfully. "There's something about class, all right, but I found out the hard way that I was just a curiosity, a play-pretty for 'em. When the ball was over, my pickup turned into a pumpkin and they went home with one of their kind in his Cadillac."

Sonny looked at J.P. for a long moment, trying to decide if J.P. was trying to tell him something. Finally he said: "See you tomorrow."

"Get a good night's rest. Go to bed early, and alone." J.P. admonished. "We've got a big day ahead of us tomorrow."

"You just have Paragon ready. I'll be here bright-eyed and bushy-tailed," Sonny replied with a touch of annoyance edging his words over J.P.'s implication and fatherly attitude.

Cathy wore a pair of form-fitting blue jeans tucked into the tops of her cowboy boots. A Navajo concho belt and turquoise pendant earrings added the Santa Fe touch to her western attire.

"Where do you want to go?" Sonny asked as they walked across the parking lot in front of the Inn.

"Let's go up towards Aerie," she suggested. "That's pretty country and surely we can find some lonely canyon with a little singing creek where we can get away from people. Is that all right with you?"

"Point the way," Sonny replied as he held open the pickup door for her.

They drove along the two-lane winding road that coursed upwards into the mountainous heart of the Mescalero Apache Reservation. The route led them along a narrow canyon through the shadows of stately evergreens, under the canopies of shimmering aspen leafs and across intermittent mountain parks with swatches of colorful flowers dotting the carpet of grass. They stopped at a log cabin restaurant in the little village of Aerie which lay in a long, open valley near the crest of the mountain range.

A little south of the village they found a two-rutted trail that headed up a small valley bisected by a sparkling creek. Sonny eased his pickup along the winding road until Cathy selected a meadow partially shaded by towering blue spruces.

Sonny took out the bed tarp he kept behind the seat and spread it out in the shade of the evergreens. Cathy opened the styrofoam containers and laid out the lunch. They settled down on the tarpaulin, Sonny cross-legged and Cathy with her legs folded under her. They lunched on fried chicken, potato salad, carrot and celery strips, black olives and potato chips, laced with sips of red wine.

The late summer sun slipped across a cloudless sky. A grasshopper whirred over the meadow and a flock of piñon jays flashed along the valley, punctuating the mountain serenity with ribald scolding. A gray, fox-eared squirrel ventured warily out of the forest to sit on its haunches on a tree stump nearby. The warm sun, the food, the wine and the peaceful setting began to have an affect on Sonny.

"Why don't you take a little nap while I put things away?" Cathy suggested.

"Why don't you join me?"

"That would be nice. Let me put the food away so the ants won't get to it." She came to snuggle beside him, leaned over and kissed him lightly on the cheek. He pillowed her head on his arm and held her to his side. Within minutes she lapsed into deep, slow, rhythmical breathing. Sonny's pulse raced at the nearness and the womanly smell of her perfume and hair. He lay there, turning over in his mind the budding attraction he felt for her, and where it might lead. The tranquility of the mountain park and Cathy at peace in his arms eased him into the dark, silent world of slumber.

Later they walked, hand-in-hand, up the valley, stopping to admire the little stream and to watch a golden eagle soar lazily on the updrafts. While Cathy gathered wildflowers, Sonny sat on a rock in the shade of a towering pine tree. He looked at his watch. They're on about the eighth race, he thought, and you know, I couldn't care less.

The trip back was leisurely. The sun slipped from the heavens toward the mountainous crest beyond the valley; but time, for Sonny, stood still. Cathy sat beside him, her hand resting on his leg. Both were at ease and small talk was interspersed by long periods of silence. Sonny's thoughts were never very far away from that delicate hand resting ever so lightly, but so electrifying, on his thigh.

As they were pulling into the parking area in front of the Inn, Cathy said: "Sonny, I don't know when I've enjoyed a day as much as I've enjoyed this one. It's a day I'll always remember and treasure. You're nice to be with. Nothing like I expected. You're different from most men I meet."

Sonny pulled into a parking space, turned off the ignition and reached to pull Cathy to him. She let him kiss her, then pulled back gently. "Will I see you tonight?" she asked.

"I was hoping you didn't have any plans," Sonny replied.

"Why don't you pick me up about seven thirty and we'll have dinner."

"I'll be here."

Cathy gathered her purse and reached up on the dash to pick up the bouquet of wildflowers.

"Your flowers wilted," Sonny observed.

"Yes," she said ruefully, "the good things of life seem to wilt and die when I touch them."

The hostess, acting on Cathy's instructions, seated them at a secluded table in a far corner of the Inn's elegant dining room. As soon as she was out of earshot, Cathy turned to Sonny and said in a petulant tone: "Why did you send me those roses?"

"Well, . . . because," Sonny replied, caught by surprise at her unexpected but apparent irritation at what he considered to be a gesture of thoughtfulness. "I thought you'd enjoy them. You seemed to be upset because the flowers you gathered this afternoon died, so I figured I'd send some roses to take their place."

"You shouldn't have done that," she said emphatically and picked up her menu.

Sonny saw the set look in her face and decided it best to let the matter drop. He could not stifle a feeling of chagrin and disappointment at a rebuff over what he thought was an act of caring.

They placed their orders with a friendly waitress then went to the salad bar. During the course of the meal Sonny studied the woman sitting across the table from him, the women he thought he was beginning to know, but now seemed so distant. He watched as she picked indifferently over her food, and pointedly avoided meeting his eyes. Other than some polite, but strained conversation, they ate in silence.

It was during after-dinner coffee that Sonny began to accept Cathy's strange behavior and her reluctance to conversation as that peculiar, unpredictable nature of women which he had never understood. He accepted it as such and let his buoyant feeling of earlier evening return. He told her about the horses that he thought might offer Paragon the most competition in tomorrow's futurity race. He explained Paragon of Merit's racing bloodline and of the young stallion's natural talent for the sport. He bragged on the horse's good disposition and how easy it was to handle. Still carrying the conversation, he said how J.P., a man that was one of the best horsemen and trainers in Sonny's opinion, had talked him into riding a maiden horse for an unknown stable. A one-horse-stable belonging to a rancher who doesn't know the horse racing industry.

It was when the waitress stopped at the table to ask if they wanted more coffee that Cathy said: "Sonny, I have a splitting headache. I'm going to my room."

It was after he had unlocked and opened her room door and returned her key that she turned and said: "Sonny, I've had a change of plans. I won't be able to see you again." She turned abruptly and started into the room.

"Wait a minute. What did I do?" Sonny exclaimed as he reached out to hold the door from being closed in his face.

"You didn't do anything. You're sweet, a nice guy. And God only knows how I appreciate that," she said. "But my plans have changed and I'll be leaving Sierra Vista in the morning."

Sonny's face flushed with sudden anger. He reached into his pocket and pulled out a crumpled greenback. "Here," he snapped as he pressed it into her hand, "call me someday when you feel like gettin' your kicks from playin' with the stable help."

"Don't! Don't say that," Cathy sobbed. She dropped the bill and turned to run into the room.

Sonny pulled the door shut with a slam and headed down the hallway.

She was packing her belongings when the telephone rang. Cathy checked the impulsive reflex to respond. Sonny could be in the lobby by now, she thought. While the right side of her brain that dictated pragmatic reasoning said: Don't answer it. Keep packing. Run. The other side, the side that heard the murmuring from an aching heart, led her to stand beside the insistent phone. She slowly picked up the receiver and put it to her ear.

"Hello, are you there?" A curt masculine voice asked.

"Yes Manny, I'm here," she replied, regretting that she had listened to her heart instead of her head.

"Did you get it done?"

"No," she mumbled.

"Tie it up tonight. I'll call you in the morning."

"No."

"What the hell you mean, no."

"No means he's gone and I won't see him again," Cathy replied with anger in her voice.

"You mean he didn't go for it?"

"I haven't ask him."

"Goddamnit," Manny growled, "you've had two days to get it done. What's the hang up?"

"I don't think he'll go for it. He's straight."

"Listen, you fuckin' broad, you aren't paid to think. And don't give me that straight shit. You think jockeys are choirboys? They got their price, like you

115

and everybody else. You tell him what it's worth to you both if Paragon doesn't win tomorrow. You got that?"

Cathy made no reply.

In an attempt at enticement, Manny continued in a bridled and somewhat condescending voice: "Hell, baby, the horse isn't favored to win. All the kid's got to do is make sure that it doesn't. Like we agreed, I put twenty-five thousand in small bills in a safety deposit box in the American Savings Bank here. It's in Alice Mackey's name and under her social security number. If anyone tries to check, they'll find a dead end. You remember, she OD'd in Mexico. Barbara saw me put the money in the box, she signed Mackey's name on the signature card and she's got the key. You can check that out with her.

"She'll be watching the race on TV. If Rogers does like you tell him, an' Paragon don't win, Barbara'll go with you to the bank, get the money and give it to you. Take your five grand cut and give the jockey twenty, like I told you.

"If the little shit lets the horse win, Barbara'll turn the money back to me. You understand?"

"It may come as a surprise to you, but not everyone can be bought," Cathy said. Then as an afterthought she said in a small voice, "just some of us."

"Listen you bitch!" Manny growled. "You don't tell me what you will do and what you won't do. You were brought here to do a simple job. That boy'll be putty if you work him right. You do whatever it takes to get it done but you get that goddamn jockey to throw the race or I'll see to it that you'll have to wear a paper sack over you face to ever lay another trick. You have until. . . ."

Cathy softly cradled the receiver. She closed and latched her suitcase and cosmetic case, picked them up and left the room.

20

Wayne put the receiver down

and stood looking at the telephone, his mind turning over the possible implications of the message that some fellow named Manny wanted to meet with him. He figured it was probably in response to his call earlier that morning to Scavarda. It had been a long shot, he figured, like drawing a card to fill an inside straight. Strictly a gamble, a nothing-ventured, nothing-gained deal prompted by Garza's threats.

The story J.P. had told him about a man eager to pay big money for a break-maiden, a novice horse, had given Wayne food for thought. Always on the alert for something or someone that might be vulnerable, like a predator on the prowl, Wayne had caught the scent of money on the table. He had deliberated on the two men involved in what J.P. had said was a deadlocked deal between Scavarda and Trainham as he would assess the strengths and weaknesses of players in a game of poker. He thought maybe he saw a possibility of dealing himself in.

According to the gossip bought by several rounds of drinks for the elbow benders and the gin rummy players in the Nineteenth Hole at the country club and some heavy tipping to bartenders at the better watering holes in the village, Wayne figured Scavarda to be a man with strong financial resources, and maybe some underworld connections back east. Like one fellow had confided to Wayne: "You gotta figure that a man from Jersey with a name like Scavarda, and with his money and those muscle men that follow him around, he's bound to be in the rackets." From what Wayne could gather, Scavarda was a man accustomed to wielding unquestioned authority, a man to whom money was power and power was supreme. He'll be a tough man to deal with, Wayne thought.

Wayne's impression, when J.P. had introduced him to Dock, was that the old cowboy was an up-front, what you see is what you got kind of man. He looked to Wayne like he ought to be with the spit-and-whittle boys at some local cow auction barn instead of here at the Downs holding a good hand in a high-stakes horse race, like a man with a pair showing in a three-card game of Taos, Wayne thought. But he'd be an easy mark in a card game, and maybe my way into this horse trade. J.P.'ll be his coach, and I've got a handle on him. Then there's Trainham's boy and my IOUs. Maybe I can parlay them as leverage against the old man and get a piece of this action.

Wayne left his room and headed for the restaurant. As he sat with coffee and a cigarette, he thought back to better times, times when he wouldn't have had to try and finagle his way into tough deals hoping to scrounge a buck, times when the club was like a money tree and he could afford to take a broad to the posh resorts in Mexico and the Caribbean. That was before the boom had faded, before the price of Texas intermediate crude had fallen from thirty-eight dollars a barrel to around ten. Wayne, like others riding the crest of the wave of prosperity and who were convinced they were in the heart of the mother lode, crashed headfirst against the jagged rocks of hard times.

Reports from his CPA showed the club operating in the red. There was no longer the need for a patron to call for reservations in the dining room. Even on a Saturday night there were more tables unoccupied than occupied. The best game that Wayne could find in town might be a five-dollar, three-raise-limit game. He found himself playing more solitaire than gin or poker. Gambling debts and bar bills were not given much priority by people who were pawning their Rolex watches and selling their Cadillacs in order to make house payments, and certainly no recognition in the allocations of the bankruptcy courts.

Those banks in the Southern Baptist belt that were fortunate enough to have funds had turned down loan requests from the owner of an exclusive club that sold liquor, was reputed to sponsor games of chance in private rooms and might even arrange for an attractive girl to entertain a visiting salesman. Wayne had even tried to solicit help from two club members who were bank directors. Both had turned a deaf ear to the request and had even stopped dropping by for their habitual after-work drink and round or two of rummy.

Wayne's search for financing had led him to El Paso where, during the course of his quest, he sat in on some back-room poker games. A word here and there put him in touch with a Mexican named Pedro Garza y Bueno who had business connections on both sides of the border but lived and operated out of Juárez. Señor Garza, over dinner at Paco Wong's Chinese Restaurant, listened to Wayne describe his dining and gambling establishment, how lucrative it had been until the oil bust, and his current need for financial backing to tide the business over until the crunch was past. Without even the suggestion of going to Midland to look into the deal, Garza offered to buy the club. Wayne balked at selling, but after a lot of tequila and arguing, a deal was finally negotiated. Garza would purchase a quarter interest in the business, at Wayne's appraisal price, and he would furnish the financing for the operation. Wayne would pay twenty per cent interest, compounded monthly, on seventy-five percent of the outstanding principal. Wayne held out for his right to buy back, at Garza's purchase price, the quarter interest when the loan was paid off. The loan was secured by an open-ended note and a mortgage on Wayne's retained three-quarter interest. Wayne left El Paso with an attaché case carrying bundled one hundred dollars bills that to Wayne, who operated on the dark side of society, carried the smell of illegal drugs.

The financial resources of those dependent on the petroleum industry continued to deteriorate. Crude from foreign countries was delivered to ports in the United States at a price that was far below what it took to produce it internally. The count of drilling rigs probing for new oil in the Permian Basin of Texas dropped from in the hundreds to the teens. Income from producing wells dropped by two-thirds as did the royalties to land owners. It was said, and not altogether in jest, that a person did not want to risk walking too close to the sides of the high-rise buildings in downtown Midland, Texas. Someone might fall on you.

Garza kept in touch over the months through telephone calls and an occasional visit by his stateside associates. There had been no demands for loan payments or an accounting, just the subtle reminders that the Mexican connection was still interested in owning the club outright.

But Wayne recalled, as he signed the breakfast tab charging it to his room, the visit three weeks ago had a different tone. Garza, accompanied by a man Wayne perceived to be a bodyguard and a blond mistress, unexpectedly showed up at the club for dinner. After they shared a congenial meal, Wayne took them on a tour of the club from the kitchen through the general dining and dancing area and to the private dining and game rooms. Wayne showed Garza the books to substantiate the fact that there had not been a profit to divide; that, in fact, the club was still losing money.

Over after-dinner brandies in the almost deserted bar the conversation had turned from social table-talk to hard-ball business. The Mexicans' fondness for courtesies and toasts to health and wealth was followed by Garza's blunt statement pressuring Wayne to relinquish his interest in the club. Wayne parried, saying he was confident that the economy would rebound soon and that he knew that he could repay the loan and buy back Garza's interest, if only given a little more time.

The Mexican sat for some minutes, idly toying with his black Cuban cigar. His eyes narrowed in concentration as he looked across the table at Wayne. Wayne was not used to a feeling of inferiority and felt his face flush in suppressed anger. Finally Garza said: *"Pues, señor,* You do not want to sell. Then you can pay me the money you owe me, no?"

Wayne looked at the smiling face, with the black mestizo eyes that were not smiling. He said: "No. You know I haven't got the money, but if you'll give me a little time, I'll damned sure pay you in full."

"Mister Belcheff," the man said with an easy shrug of his shoulders and a disarming smile. "You have thirty days, *amigo,* then my lawyer will be here to settle our account, or negotiate a foreclosure." He pushed his chair back and stood. He motioned his head at his companions and turned to leave. *"Buenos noches, señor Belcheff,"* he said as he reached to pat the blond on her shapely derriere. *"Hasta la vista."*

21

Dock woke gently. He rolled over onto his back, staring into the dark room, trying to recall the fading details of the dream that had awakened him. As best he could remember, it had something to do with he and Mario working cattle in a corral somewhere. He used to wonder if his dreams might be some kind of a prediction, his subconscious mind trying to tell him something. He had read where Indians would fast for days and then have dreams that had meaning to them. But for Dock, dreams were just nonsensical, nebulous scenes without rhyme or reason that faded with the night at sunrise. He rolled over to look at the digital clock on the bedside table. The red figures stood at 4:10.

Today would be the big day. Further sleep was out of the question, so rather than lie there, tossing and turning, Dock swung his legs out from under the sheet to grope for his houseshoes. He rose, stretched and stepped over to the picture window to pull open the drapes. On the channel seven TV news from Albuquerque last evening a pretty, blond-headed young weather person had prognosticated that Sunday in the Land of Enchantment would be a beautiful Indian summer day with a chance for showers in the higher elevations. Dock could see stars twinkling in a heaven that was beginning to show a tinge of gray silhouetting the black mountains to the west. He was relieved. A muddy track would have made a difference. Raised in west Texas, Paragon sure never had much experience running in mud, Dock thought as he turned from the window and headed for the bathroom.

He was at the barn in time to help J.P. put out the morning feed. They were sitting in camp chairs in front of the stall watching Paragon eat as the blazing rim of the sun rose above the piney foothills down the valley. J.P. was smoking a cigarette and Dock was fighting the want-to.

Dock had smoked for over twenty years, going back to his days as a young cowpuncher when a nickel sack of Bull Durham smoking tobacco would last him a week, then to later years when he would smoke his way through two packs of tailor-mades a day. Martha had the persistence and zeal of Carrie Nation when it came to crusading against tobacco. During their courtship and after marriage, Dock, like the Marlboro Man, had held to his rights to smoke. Little by little he surrendered: first agreeing to not smoke in the house, then limiting himself to a pack a day, then finally, her pleading compounded by the much publicized threats to smokers of lung cancer, moved him to give her his promise to give up the 'nasty habit', as she described it. But the craving still remained, especially after a good meal, or when he was nervous and tense, like he was this morning. But, as he told himself, to give in, to scratch the itch, would leave him with a feeling of weakness for yielding and the guilt of going back on his word to Martha now that she wasn't here to argue her cause. He fought to dismiss the urge by turning his thoughts to the upcoming Oklahoma Futurity scheduled as the tenth race on the afternoon's program.

The dark green of the mountains that harbored the valley and Sierra Vista Downs made a contrasting horizon against the pale blue sky of midday, which was without a blemish save for an occasional contrail from a passing jet. Post time for the first race was set for one thirty. Since before noon, cars coming east along the four-lane highway from the village to the track entrance were strung out bumper-to-bumper.

The mood of the crowd in the grandstand on racing days was a blending of festivity, leisure and anticipation. The backside was an admixture of bustling activity and the suspense of nervous waiting. This would be a busy afternoon for trainers, jockeys and stable hands. Horses would be made ready for the moment when the loud speaker from the steward's stand would announce their race and the trumpeter sound the Call To The Post. The mounted jockeys, wearing the silks of their stable they were riding for, would be led by pony horses from the paddock to parade in front of the grandstand and on to the starting gate.

I feel about as useless as tits on a boar hog, Dock thought as he stood by watching J.P. pick up each of Paragon's hooves to check the set of the aluminum racing plates. "What can I do to help?" Dock asked.

"Nothin'," J.P. replied as he stepped back to look at the stallion, which stood nonchalant and hip-shot, the sun glistening on his black, satiny coat. "Win or lose today," J.P. drawled, "that's a helluva horse. Most track horses, especially those carrying some thoroughbred blood, tend to be high-strung. But this son-of-a-gun has the best disposition I've ever worked with. He just doesn't get excited. Not even when he's loaded into the starting gate and knows he's about to run. You've seen him Dock, he walks into the chute just like he's walking into his stall for a bait of feed. Then he just stands there. He doesn't fight it. The only sign he knows something's up is his ears are perked up and he's alert. Dock, if he can pass on to his progeny his running ability and his temperament, he'll make a whale of a standing stud. Who knows, he may go down in racing history. We can say we knew him when," J.P. finished with a chuckle.

"Well," Dock drawled, "I'll follow my mother's advise and give you your bouquet of roses now while you can smell 'em. Horses are the reflections of the people who handle 'em. Nervous, high-strung people beget nervous, high-strung horses. As they say: like begets like. I lay it to you, and the way you've handled the colt, that Paragon is sensible and has such a good disposition. You took the way the horse was bred and you accentuated the strong points. You have a way with horses, J.P., and I can tell by watching a horse's reaction to you that you smell right to them. And you're a topnotch trainer, to boot."

"Thanks, Dock," J.P. responded, an inflection of humble gratitude in his voice. "I take that as a real compliment, coming from a horseman like your-self."

J.P. moved over to stand beside Paragon. With his left hand resting on the horse's hip, his right hand moved to stroke the muscled croup. He worked his hand down along the back of the left leg, then moved to gently scratch the horse along the seam of its buttock. "Dock," he said slowly as he petted the horse, "you've been a mighty fine man to work for. From where I stand, you're more than my boss. I count you among the very few I call tried-and-true friends. I've heard it said that if a man has five true friends he can consider himself among the fortunate. Well, I don't believe I can muster five, but I'd sure like to figure you for one." He stopped messing with the horse and turned to look at his employer. "I've told you before, but I'll tell you again. I'll always owe you and Ross a debt of gratitude for giving me another chance."

"Well," Dock responded, "we just eared the horse down for you. You got on and made the ride with your own determination and grit. I imagine your struggle against booze is kind of like my fight to stop smoking. All the well-intentioned, good advice didn't do anything to change my desires. If anything, it rubbed against my stubborn streak. It was only when I realized I had a cause that I decided I wanted to quit, and did."

"Tobacco and booze," J.P. said. "Both bad habits and hell to kick. Maybe someday I'll try to follow your example and throw my cigarettes in the trash. But for now, it's one step and one day at a time. I guess we'd better start on over toward the paddock. They'll be calling the tenth race pretty soon."

J.P. untied Paragon's halter rope from the tie-ring mounted on the barn wall and with Dock and Robert walking behind, they started up the gravelly trail leading to the track. They left the barn area and entered the underpass at the southeast side of the oval track. The sound of Paragon's shod hooves treading on the concrete slab echoed off the concrete walls. As they left the tunnel and came up into the area inside of the track, Dock looked up at the grandstand. Gay pennants lined the eaves of the overhang covering the grandstand and fluttered in the afternoon breezes. The parking lot on the slope above the track was filled to capacity. The sight of the milling people who packed the three-tiered stands and the exciting voice coming over the public address system calling the ninth race began to erode Dock's self-willed composure. The butterflies in his guts, which he had fought to suppress since early morning, took flight.

Dock glanced sideways at J.P. He looks like he might be going for a Sunday afternoon stroll in the park, Dock thought. I've got a lot riding on this race but not as much as he has. Regardless of what happens in the next few minutes, I've got to be thinking about going back to the ranch. What I end up doing with Paragon just depends. I might sell him. If the horse has it in him like J.P. thinks, it doesn't belong in a ranch remuda. I could leave it on the track but that would cost money. Even good ones don't always run in the money. I guess I'll cross that bridge when I get to it. But J.P.'s riding the comeback trail on Paragon, both with his way of making a living and with his family, and I'm not sure he's on firm ground yet. Even if I was to leave Paragon on the track, with him as a trainer, bucking the odds on racing, like they are, he probably couldn't make a living with only one horse. He's got a ways to go to prove to himself, his wife and other horse people that he's recovered and got control before he'll attract a stable of horses. He doesn't look it, walking so seemingly unconcerned, but he's bound to be wound up tighter than an eight-day clock.

The ninth race had been run. The winning horse, with the jockey up, was in the winner's circle, flanked by the owners and the trainer, receiving the garland of roses and the winner's blanket. The also-rans had been unsaddled in the paddock and were being led across the grassy oval inside the track, back towards the barns, to pass alongside the oncoming contenders for the tenth race. Dock stepped aside from the pathway to make room for the returning horses, then moved in again to walk along behind Paragon. A feeling of pride welled up in his mind as he admired the horse's conformation and the muscles that flexed to ripple under a shiny jet coat. He saw in his minds eye, Martha, on her knees, holding the baby colt up to where it could nurse the old mare. He thought of how proud she would be at this moment, and a lump rose in his throat.

The half-circle paddock facing the grandstand was situated just inside the oval track and east of the tote board. J.P. led Paragon to their assigned stall to meet Sonny coming from the jockeys' dressing room carrying his saddle and wearing Dock's blue on white silk blouse with the Lazy DT Connected (♑) brand on the back and the number seven on his right shoulder. Dock stood to one side and watched as J.P., Robert and Sonny readied the horse. He looked over the other nine contenders as they were being brought in and saddled. Rebel, the handicappers' favorite, was a solid brown, leggy, long-muscled stallion. Maybe the odds-makers are right, Dock thought. He ought to be able to push the track behind him with that powerful rear end and driving slope to his croup.

Bright Babe, the handicappers' second choice, was a classy-looking, refined little sorrel filly with a star in her forehead. Dock judged that she stood a full hand under Rebel and half a hand smaller than Paragon. She had a textbook conformation for a sprinter quarter horse: the barrel chest, heavy-muscled forearms and power-packed hips. The racing history of her dam and sire, and their get, including Bright Babe's own speed index, was impressive enough to make her an odds-on favorite with horse racing enthusiasts.

Gray Badger, a long-legged, long-backed, angular, flea- bitten gray filly reminded Dock of a drawing he had seen of Don Quixote's horse, Rocinante. She doesn't have an ounce of fat on her, Dock thought. She's so rough she's kinda ugly, but she beat us in the trials, and she'll be a tough contender today.

There was something about the Halleluja horse that caught Dock's eye as it was led past Paragon's stall. Dock stepped out to study the stallion as it moved down the line toward a stall. The handicappers had set the horse in at 25 to 1 odds—the long shot of the field. Dock remembered watching the horse in the trial run when it placed fourth. He had mentioned to J.P. that it had a long reach and a lot of drive, but just seemed to be coasting, not really driving for the finish line like it should. J.P. had said that the horse was from Florida and that the trial run was its first time out, here. He had gone on to say that Halleluja's people probably wanted to keep the horse under wraps until one of the big races. "You can put your money down on one thing," J.P. had commented as he and Dock had watched the trainer lead Halleluja off the track after the trial run, "they didn't spend the money it cost to haul the horse and their people all the way up here from Florida and pay the late nomination fee for the futurity without knowing they had a strong contender."

J.P. busied himself seeing that Sonny's saddle was set just right, that there were no wrinkles in the saddle pad and that the girth was tightened snug, but not so tight as to constrict. There was no need for him to be studying the other nine horses being put under the saddles. He had spent hours during the past week of trial runs studying the qualifying horses and their past performances. As a horseman and trainer he well knew that an animal's actions and its reactions to stimuli have a certain amount of predictability. J.P. had first learned the certainty of this as a professional rodeo cowboy. As a contestant, he had studied and made detailed notes on the actions of each animal in the major rodeo strings. When he was getting down on a bull or bucking horse in the chute, he knew how that animal was going to react when the chute gate flew open and his mount exploded into the arena. Some bulls bucked in a tight circle, some spinning to the left, some to the right. Some bucked straight away. Some horses left the chute on a short hard run, to stop suddenly, jobbing their front feet into the tanbark of the arena and burying their head down between their front legs as they broke in two, or turned the crank, as the cowboys say. But for the most part, a savvy rider could anticipate his mounts actions and ride to counteract.

J.P. knew there was a like predictability to horses on the track. When contenders were led up to the starting gate, each animal senses what is ahead. Some that are high-strung can be counted on to become fractious, fighting their handlers and the starting gate, sapping their energies before the race. Others, nine times out of ten, will walk right into their gate with little or no trouble. When the bell sounds and the gates snap open, the horses are trained to lunge out of the chute and break into a dead run. On a short sprint, two furlongs or less, a poor start coming out of the gate can cost a contender the race. In the crowded field racing for a finish line, the quirks of some horses detract from their running performance.

Not all trainers show the same rapport with horses, nor are they all equal in training abilities. And not all jockeys are on a par when it comes to guiding a horse to the best advantage in a field of running horses, nor at getting the most out of their mount.

J.P. had taken all this into account on the Oklahoma Futurity contenders, their trainers, and the jockeys, to figure Paragon's competition and how best to run the race. J.P., Sonny and Dock had gathered in Dock's motel room to plan their strategy for the race. J.P. had taken each one of the contenders and described the likelihood of how that horse and jockey would perform. He had instructed Sonny on defensive and offensive maneuvers, based on what might be expected from the other horses. The race was to be a four hundred and forty yard straight-away, figured to be run in twenty-one to twenty-two seconds. A slow or bad break from the gate, being bumped or bumping another horse and thrown off stride, veering, breaking over, or any number of mishaps or accidents that might cause a horse to fall behind a fraction of a second would be the difference between running in the money, or driving in the winners.

J.P. stood by Paragon's head, absent-mindedly stroking the horse beneath the jaw. His mind kept trying to review, working to remember if he had done a thorough job of researching and had covered everything with Sonny. He struggled against the resurfacing doubts, forcing his mind to dismiss them. He knew Paragon was conditioned and ready. He knew he had studied, from every angle, the probable performance of his horse and the other nine, that he had covered these possibilities with Sonny, and that Sonny knew and understood just how J.P. wanted him to handle his mount. J.P. knew the advantage of Sonny and Paragon having raced together before and that they were a team, a pair, a combination that should be hard to beat.

In spite of what he knew to be their advantages: Paragon's competitive spirit, his speed and handling ease, his own training ability and knowledge of the racing game and Sonny's ability and experience as a jockey; facts that in the core of J.P.'s mind were irrefutable, his palms were moist and his stomach felt like it was sucked up against his diaphragm, making it hard to breath. Well, he thought, it'll all be history in a few minutes.

22

The announcement blared out

from loud speakers positioned at each end of the grandstand as trailing notes from a trumpet echoed back from the surrounding mountains:

> The "Call To The Post" has sounded for the tenth race, the Oklahoma Futurity, the second jewel in the Sierra Vista Triple Crown for Quarter Horses. Ten horses will be competing in a four hundred and forty yard sprint for the seven hundred and fifty thousand dollar purse. This allowance will offer quinella and exacta wagering. In the tenth race we have no changes or corrections on the program. Post time in ten minutes.

A man wearing a broad-brimmed Stetson, leather chaps over Levis and riding a stock saddle rode a sorrel gelding into the paddock area to rein up in front of Paragon's stall. J.P. snapped the rider's lead shank to the ring of Paragon's snaffle bit, then gave Sonny a leg-up to mount. As the mounted man led Paragon onto the track, Sonny tightened the chin strap on his crash helmet. The black stallion pranced alongside the restraining pony horse as it reacted in excitement over being in the company of other horses and sensing the upcoming race.

Dock and J.P. left the paddock after the last horse had been led out. They walked over to stand with other horsemen at the rail of the viewing stand. The digital clock on the tote board read 5:22. The sun stood about an hour above the crest of the mountain and the high altitude coolness that came with the elongating shadows had the matronly ladies in the Jockey Club reaching for their shoulder wraps.

The ponied horses, with their jockeys up, paraded west along the groomed track fronting the grandstand, then turned, and in a trot passed back in front of the stand toward the starting gate that lay across a straight-away extension intersecting the east end of the oval track. Sonny took the slack out of the rein, exerting a slight pull to lay the port of the snaffle bit against the bars in Paragon's mouth. He could feel the horse's eagerness in the tugs on the rein as Paragon pulled against the bit and in the choppy gait as the horse danced sideways as it tried to move away from the restricting pony horse.

Sonny wanted to win this race. He wanted to win it for Dock and J.P. He wanted to jockey Paragon to run the race he knew the horse was capable of running. But above all, he wanted to win this race for Sonny. For the first time that he could recall it wasn't for the money or his standing in the jockeys' ratings. It was for that moment in the winner's circle before the TV cameras and photographers. The recognition of not only being a winning jockey, but one that had the distinction and acclaim of booting his mount across the finish line ahead of the field, capturing two jewels of the Triple Crown.

Wherever she was, Sonny wanted the satisfaction of knowing that Cathy would know, that she would see the pictures in the newspaper and on television of him mounted on Paragon of Merit receiving the garland of roses and winner's blanket, surrounded by important people looking up to him. Not just a paid boy who rode horses for a living, but a man that was rated at the top in his field. These were the mental images that occupied Sonny's mind and set his jaw in determination as he approached the starting gate.

A drawing, prior to the race, positioned each horse to its place in the starting gate. Gatemen, each assigned a horse, received their horse from the pony rider. They ran a short rein through the right ring of the snaffle bit and, at the word from the starter, led their horses into the narrow confines of the starting gate to stand behind the spring-loaded gates. Each gateman hoisted himself up to stand on a little platform beside the horse's head where he could, by his hold on the strap threaded through the ring on the snaffle bit, control the movement of the horse's head. Paragon, running as the number seven horse, was in the seventh gate away from the inside track rail.

J.P. raised his binoculars and adjusted them to bring the horses and handlers into clear focus. "He's doin' fine," he said to Dock in a quiet voice of guarded optimism.

The noise from the grandstand slowly subsided as spectators craned their necks, looking eastward up the track in anticipation of the starting bell. Dock's hands took a tight grip on the railing. His breathing became rapid and shallow.

"They're having trouble with Bright Babe," J.P. said as he studied the starting gate through field glasses. "She's got her head down. Musta jerked away from the gateman. He's reaching down trying to get hold of. . . Oh shit, she threw her head up!" J.P. exclaimed. "Hit the gateman right in the face."

Dock had seen Bright Babe's gateman suddenly straighten up from where he was bent over trying to get hold of the cheek strap of the horse's bridle. The man's hat flew off as he reared back and put both hands to cover his face.

"She's rearing," J.P. exclaimed. "Tryin' to go over backwards. The jockey's down an' she's got him pinned against the back gate. Damn, they're in a jam!" J.P. swung the binoculars over to check on Paragon behind gate seven, two away from Bright Babe. The disturbance had sent a wave of uneasiness over the other horses. Some began to move backwards, ramming their butts against the end gate, then fighting their heads and surging forward, fighting the restraining chutes and the gatemen trying to hold them. "Goddamnit," J.P. growled, "why in hell don't they open the gate and let her back out before they get in real trouble?"

Just as he asked the question the gate behind Bright Babe opened and the horse struggled in the narrow confines of the chute to get her feet under her. She did, then charged out backward. Two or three steps out of the gate and her thrusting, struggling back feet slipped in the soft turf, her butt went down and she fell over backwards and to one side, throwing the jockey off. Several track employees ran to the thrashing animal. One man grabbed hold of the rein.

The sorrel filly fought to stand. On her feet, she shook her head and blew forcibly through flared nostrils. The man holding the rein turned to lead her in a circle. It was then that J.P., watching through his binoculars, gave a slow, low whistle. He said to Dock: "Sure as hell, she broke her right hind leg. Can you see how she's packin' that leg? It's broke right there below the hock. Damn, that's tough luck!" he exclaimed.

A wave of compassion shadowed Dock and he slowly shook his head in sympathy for the little horse as he noticed her holding her right leg up while that part of the leg just below the hock hung at an unnatural angle. The word was sent from the stewards' box, and gates behind the other nine horses swung open and the gatemen backed them out. The murmur of voices and the hubbub of activity in the grandstand rose as people tried to figure what had happened and what was going on behind the starting gate.

"They won't call the race, will they?" Dock asked.

"No, the track vet will disqualify Bright Babe. There'll be an announcement made for all those holding tickets on her to go turn 'em in, or exchange 'em for a ticket on another horse. There'll probably be about a twenty minute delay before they call the horses back to the starting gate. It means we'll have to sweat it out a little longer," J.P. said as he ground out a cigarette butt under his boot and shook a replacement out of his pack.

A tractor towing a livestock trailer pulled onto the track and made its way to where a crowd was gathering around the sorrel filly. The driver maneuvered the tractor to spot the rear of the trailer just in front of the crippled horse. They opened the trailer gate and the man holding the rein moved to lead the horse up into the trailer. Dock winced inwardly as he saw the filly lurch forward, hobbling on three legs. He sorrowed for the horse as he imagined the broken bones grinding against sensitive nerves; and felt for the owner and trainer, people who were no doubt devastated over this stroke of bad luck and knew the horse, in which they had invested so much care, time and money would have to be put down.

The nine horses were back in the starting gate. J.P. had his field glasses trained on gate seven. The announcement came over the public address system: "They're ready to race!" There was a slight pause, a loud ringing of a buzzer and the announcer's rapid-fire calling of the race:

Here they come! A clean break. It's Rebel to take the early lead on the inside. On the extreme outside it's Gray Badger showing speed. Hallelujah and Paragon of Merit making their move in the center of the field. It's Hallelujah and Paragon of Merit moving to the front with Rebel and Gray Badger trailing by half a length. It's Hallelujah in the lead by a neck. Paragon of Merit's movin' up as Rogers goes to the bat. Paragon of Merit's moving out ahead! It's Paragon of Merit by a nose over Hallelujah with Gray Badger trailing by half a length.

Most of the spectators in the grandstand had risen to their feet as a wave of excitement swept over the crowd. Dock looked at J.P., who had followed the race with his field glasses. "What do you think?" he asked.

"It'll be a photo finish," J.P. replied, "but from this angle, it sure looked like our horse forged ahead after Sonny went to the bat."

After a brief pause during which the officials studied the slow-motion video of the race, the announcer's voice boomed out over the clamor of the bettors:

Paragon of Merit, owned by Dock Trainham of Horsehead Crossing, Texas, trained by J.P. Bates, and ridden by Sonny Rogers is the official winner, by a nose, of the Oklahoma Futurity. In second place it's Hallelujah, owned by the Okeechobee Stables of Clewiston, Florida, trained by Victor Smith, with jockey Art LeBlanc in the silks. In third place it's Gray Badger owned by Sam Flowers and ridden by Rudy Gonzales. Running in fourth place, Rebel, the horse favored by many to win the race. The time on a fast track, with a tail wind, twenty-one and fifty-six one hundredths seconds. The odds on Paragon of Merit at the close of betting was six dollars and ten cents. He paid fourteen twenty to win, seven twenty to place and three sixty to show. Hallelujah closed the books with eleven eighty odds. He paid eleven sixty to place and six twenty to show. Gray Badger carried odds of four twenty and paid four twenty. Coming into the winner's circle is Mister Trainham with J.P. Bates leading Paragon of Merit, Sonny Rogers in the saddle. Ladies and gentlemen, having won the Texas Futurity and now the Oklahoma Futurity, Paragon of Merit is a strong contender to be the second horse in the history of Sierra Vista Downs to win the Triple Crown.

Most of the people in the grandstand were on their feet, some watching the presentation in the winner's circle, some headed for the windows to cash in a ticket on the tenth race and some to lay a bet on the eleventh. Glancing up at the crowd, Dock said to himself: "The last time I felt this shaky and weak in the knees was at the ranch when I got down off that Yellow Dog horse after he'd tried to buck me off, and came mighty close to doing it."

J.P. walked beside Paragon as Sonny reined the blowing horse into the circle of dignitaries and news media waiting for them. "I'm comin', Virginia," he said under his breath. "We did it."

Sonny sat erect on the sweating, heaving horse while the wife of the owner of the track placed a horseshoe-shaped garland of red and yellow roses over Paragon's withers. Sonny looked straight into the eyes of the cameras and mouthed behind a forced smile: "It's me, Catherine, you remember, the fellow who wasn't good enough for you and your silk-stocking crowd."

23

The last two races on that Sunday afternoon were apparently of no interest to certain people who had watched the tenth race with intent interest.

For Dock, J.P. and Sonny, there had only been the one race on the card, and they had won it. Dock and J.P. followed along behind as Robert led Paragon from the paddock to the barn area. Sonny took his saddle and headed along the walkway that led to the jockeys' dressing room.

Three men dressed in slacks and sport shirts and wearing expensive loafers accepted their winnings from the Jockey Club attendant who had cashed in their tickets on the number seven horse. They left the private box and went to a corner table in the cocktail lounge. After a waitress had brought their drinks, they huddled over the table and became engrossed in muted conversation. The oldest of the trio seemed to be doing most of the talking. He would punctuate his words with emphatic gestures, taking the cigar from his mouth to drive home a point.

Two men, one nattily dressed and with a ranchman's Panama hat sat at a rakish angle, the other wearing cowboy boots and a western-styled straw hat set square and low on his head stood together in the line of people waiting in front of a pari-mutuel window to cash in winnings tickets. During the eleventh race they huddled in guarded conversation at the far end of the Turf Club bar.

A young man with collar-length blond hair, wearing a T-shirt and faded denim trousers, left the track front section of the general admission area of the grandstand. He walked into the cavernous concrete-and-steel section under the bleachers to stand at the crowded bar. The bartender took his order for a Coors beer. He stood with one run-over, scuffed cowboy boot hooked on the bar rail and both elbows resting on the bar. He interrupted his apparent intense thoughtfulness with occasional draughts of beer from the bottle.

Dock had made reservations for three in the main dining room of the White Mountain Inn. It was his way of saying thanks to J.P. and Sonny for a job well done. A victory celebration. But each of the trio, as they sat in conversation recounting the futurity while they waited to be served, were in their innermost thoughts, realizing more than the sweet taste of victory.

Dock nursed a bourbon and water. At times he became so immersed in his personal thoughts he would lose the trend of the conversation. He had spent the hour, before he went to pick up J.P. and Sonny, in his room with a pencil and paper. The way it had figured, after J.P.'s twenty percent and Sonny's ten percent cuts of the winnings were deducted, after the IRS's cut of his share of the purse and all his outstanding accounts were paid, he should have enough left to almost pay off the money he had borrowed from Martha's estate. Then, if the calves weighed what he thought they would come fall and the market held, he could pay the loan off and clear the lien against the ranch. That would be a worry off my mind, he thought as he motioned to the waitress for another bourbon. Especially now that Patrick's making an issue of it.

J.P. sipped on his coffee, and although he held up his end of the conversation, with only an occasional lapse, his thoughts were on a promising tomorrow. He had called Virginia right after the race. She said she and Lynn had watched it on simulcast and how proud they were of him. They talked for almost an hour, planning the reunion and their lives as a family together again. They agreed that Lynn would need a room of her own now so they'd want to find a nice, furnished two-bedroom house to rent. And J.P. had told Virginia that he wanted them to buy some new clothes and the stuff that make women and young girls happy. J.P. would trade in the old Chevy pickup on one with a crew cab. It would work for a family and he could haul feed and his horseman's gear in the bed. J.P. had to struggle there in the fancy dining room to maintain his stoic composure as his mind fantasized on a bright tomorrow.

Sonny considered his part of the purse and how it would go a long way, especially with the money he already had in savings, to see him through from jockeying horses until he could get established as a trainer. But the thoughts that were paramount on his mind that evening were those of Catherine, the woman he had been so proud to have on his arm and who had made him feel a little superior to the other men that night at Barbara's party. The bronzed woman, in her white swimming suit at the pool and in her cocktail dress walking through the hotel lobby, that had turned men's heads for a second look. Cathy and her picnic. He mused over the unexpected phone call he had received earlier that evening. A woman had asked to speak to Sonny Rogers. When he acknowledged, she said, "I have a telegram for you. Would you like me to read it?" When he had answered in the affirmative, she read: "Sonny. Congratulations on a great ride. Please forgive me. I care." The lady said that it was only signed with the initial C. If he wanted a copy he could pick it up at the bus depot.

Mondays were slow on the backside. The horse people relaxed after the rigors of four straight days of racing. Marvin Yeager had been watching his people groom the horses when he received the telephone call. It was Manny telling him that the boss wanted to see him. He left instructions for the head groom to have the crew finish with the horses, put them on the walker, and then clean and re-bed the stalls while he was gone.

When he circled his pickup on the drive in front of the house, he saw Mister Scavarda waiting on the front porch. "Good morning," Marvin greeted as he climbed out of the truck and stepped up the red flagstone step to stand in front of the older man.

"Good morning," Scavarda responded. "Sit down," he said and indicated the chair beside him. "Coffee?" he asked.

"No thanks," Marvin replied as he took the seat. "I've had my quota for this morning."

"I've been thinking about Trainham's horse," Scavarda said. "I guess I should have listened to you. I checked out the cowboy when you were so hot to buy his horse. I found out that he needed money. He had a loan that was crowding him. If I'd sweetened my offer some I'd a probably bought the horse. But that's water under the bridge. The win yesterday should get Trainham out of hock, at least it'll get the bank off his back for a while.

"I've made some calls," Scavarda continued. "I've interested some people in syndicating the horse. That is if we can get Trainham to sell. What do you think?"

"Well,"Yeager replied thoughtfully, "whatever price Mister Trainham might have put on his horse before yesterday won't buy it today. He may not be up on the value of horse flesh in the racing industry, but I know he listens to

Bates who knows the value of good horses. I don't think Bates will stand by and let someone steal the horse. There'll be a lot of interest in a horse that's won two futurities, and should it win the third there's no tellin' what that stallion would be worth. Not only to track people but as a foundation sire for breeders."

"What're his chances in the Rainbow?" Scavarda asked.

"Based on the times he's posted and the way he handles, I'd say his chances are good for a place in the field. What he does in the Rainbow will depend on the competition. Of course, there's always the possibility he won't qualify, or if he makes the big race he might not perform. Horses have their off days, or something could happen to him during one of the runs. Who knows?"

"Like you say, who knows? Something could happen to the horse, to Trainham, to Bates, or to the jockey between now and then," Scavarda said as he unwrapped the cellophane wrapping on a cigar. "That would make a difference, wouldn't it?" he asked, more as a statement than a question.

The Wednesday night special in the motel restaurant was chicken-fried steak, Dock's favorite. He had just returned to his table from a visit to the salad bar when Ross Malone bulled his way through the crowded dining room to come and stand beside Dock's table.

Dock had noticed his approach and sensed something was wrong. It took just a closer look, as Ross stood over him, to see that the man had been drinking and, judging by the scowl on his face, was on the prod about something.

"Hello, Ross. Sit down, an' I'll buy your supper," Dock invited, indicating a chair with a thrust of his chin.

"You ought to be able to afford to," Ross said. "You've made a killin' with that black horse. But by God you damned near got beat," he growled.

Dock could see the other diners looking their way, attracted by Ross's loud and belligerent tone. "Hallelujah and Gray Badger are both tough competitors," Dock replied in a quiet voice. "Sit down, Ross an' we'll visit."

"I don't want to sit down, but I want to tell you, by rights, I ought to be the one runnin' that horse here," Ross slurred, his voice carrying across the dining room. "If it hadn't been for me tellin' you what you had, you'd a cut him; you'd a made a goddamn saddle horse out of him. An' who was it steered you to J.P.? It was me! If it hadn't a been for me, Trainham, you'd be sittin' on your butt

136

back at the ranch, scrabblin' for a living' off a hand full of ole cows, an' J.P. would be cleanin' stalls for someone when he wasn't layin' drunk in the gutter. Both you sons-a-bitches owe me a favor, an' by God I aim to collect."

Dock felt his neck stiffen and his face flush as he angered over Ross's tirade and the embarrassment he felt at the attention directed their way from families offended by Ross's language. He said in a low but firm voice: "Ross, don't use that kinda language here in front of these women and children. If you want to talk to me, sit down and we'll talk like civilized men. Or if you'd rather, we can step outside where we can discuss any problems you've got, man to man, without an audience."

Ross stood wavering in his boots, glaring down at Dock. The granite-like set to Dock's jaw and the fire in his eyes must have penetrated the whiskey fog with a message. Ross snarled: "I'll see you around." He turned and stalked out of the room while the diners divided their looks between him and Dock, who had resumed eating his salad with a hand that quivered.

24

J.P. was washing the supper dishes when the phone rang. Dock had just left the apartment headed for the motel and J.P. was not expecting a call. His first reaction to the insistent summons was one of uncertainty and apprehension. As he walked from the kitchen to the living room he thought: Could this be Virginia calling to say she's changed her mind about us getting together again, or maybe something's wrong at the barn? He picked up the phone. "Hello," he said hesitantly.

"J.P., this is Ross Malone."

A wave of relief swept over J.P. It was not Virginia and not a problem at the track. Just an old friend, probably wants to know how I see one of tomorrow's races, he thought. "Hello Ross, how are you?"

"I've seen better days," Ross replied. "Cattle business has gone to hell in a handcart. Market's down an' the range country's dryer than a popcorn fart. I think it's forgot how to rain. Us country buyers are getting crowded out of business. My old customers are either sending their cattle to the auctions in town or selling 'em on this shittin' new video thing. The cattle I've had on feed this year have come out short fifty dollars a head of breaking even. My banker's sending me dunning letters by registered mail and I haven't hit a good lick here at the track all summer. But shit, J.P., other than that everything's just lovely. How's it with you?"

J.P. laughed, then said: "Well, thanks to you for remembering me and recommending me to Mister Trainham, things are looking up. I'm sure you've been following Dock's horse."

"That's what I want to talk to you about," Ross said. "I'm over here at the Paddock with some friends. We'd like you to come join us. We've got a proposition that ought to interest you, one I think you'd be a fool not to go with."

J.P. could envision Ross and some never-sweats sitting at a corner table with their heads together scheming some way to turn an easy dollar. Years of listening to those kind of propositions that float around the backside had taught J.P. that ninety-nine percent of those sure-fire big deals were sucker bait. "Ross, it's good to hear from you and I appreciate you considering me, but I can't make it. I'm getting ready to go out to the track."

"Hold on a minute," Ross argued, "I think once you've heard what we've got in mind you'll take a little detour and come meet these people. J.P., my friends and I are planning to syndicate a horse; it's a horse you know. It'll be a big deal with big stakes down the road a ways. I've convinced 'em that you're our man to train and manage the horse. What do you say?"

"Bull shit's what I say," J.P. said to himself. "Ross," he replied, "you know I'm committed to Trainham. I won't even consider taking on another horse until after the season here. And then it would all depend on what Dock plans to do with Paragon."

"If we decide to buy the horse we've got in mind, you won't have those problems," Ross said.

"What do you mean?" J.P. asked.

"I mean we're aimin' to buy Paragon."

J.P. was taken completely by surprise. He stood there, the phone held to his ear and a puzzled frown creasing his brow.

"You there?" Ross spoke.

"Yeah, I'm here," J.P. replied slowly.

"J.P., we need you in on this deal. We need you to help swing it. We need you to work on Dock for us, and we need you to go on with the horse. As you said a minute ago, I gave you a leg up when you needed it, didn't I? An' now I want to cash in that ticket."

"Well, yeah, you put in a good word for me," J.P. agreed.

Ross continued: "You and I know Dock doesn't know a shittin' thing about the value of a horse beyond what a ranch horse is worth. He'll rely on you to tell him what price he ought to put on Paragon. We're willing to pay a fair price, but we don't want Dock to set some figure that's plumb out of reason. So, when he asks you, you suggest the price we've set. All right?"

"Have you talked to Dock?" J.P. asked

"No, we're just gettin' the deal put together," Ross replied. "I know Dock, J.P. I've bought his cattle for years. He's like a fish out of water here. He hasn't stepped in any cow shit since he left the ranch and I figure he's chomping at the bit to get back out there. If we put the right deal to him I figure he'll jump at the chance to gather his money, marbles and chalk and head for home."

Ross's cocksure attitude was beginning to irritate J.P. "I think you're wrong," he said. "Dock's already turned down a strong offer. He told me that he didn't want to sell the horse. I'd bet the horse still isn't for sale. Ross, we're looking at a two-time winner, with the possibility of winnin' a third. That'd put Paragon in The Hall of Champions, you know.

"An' you're wrong on another thing," J.P.'s tone of voice was becoming emphatic, and his words pointed. "I'm not for sale either. If you think I'm in your debt, you just wiped the slate clean by suggesting that I'd even consider working against Dock."

"Now wait a minute," Ross growled. "Don't get your shit hot. We're even considerin' cutting you in on the syndicate, without you havin' to buy in. I didn't ask you to renege on your deal with Dock, just to convince him that our offer for Paragon is a good one; and that he ought to take it, go tend to his cows and leave the running of horses on the track to racing people."

"Ross," J.P. retorted, "Dock and I've agreed that he should play out this hand, at least through the Rainbow. After two good purses I don't think he's in a financial bind, so I wouldn't figure on that leverage if I were you and your playmates." J.P.'s temper began to reach the boiling point. His voice rose and the delivery was clipped as he continued: "You must figure me an' Dock are a couple of dumb-asses. You think you can con me into hoodwinkin' Dock, and him sucker enough to play your game. Well, Ross, that's a bunch of bull shit. You an' your fuckin' friends can stick your idea of stealing Paragon up your syndicated asses!" J.P. slammed down the phone, pulled a cigarette out of a pack and with trembling hands struck a match and lit the smoke.

Wayne had to hunt Patrick down. He looked for him in the bars, where some bartenders said yes, they'd served someone fitting the description but hadn't seen him lately. Finally the trail led to The Barn, where a string band backed by amplifiers turned too high assaulted patrons with country and western music. Wayne spent the better part of three nights sitting in a corner table waiting and watching. It was Friday night about ten o'clock when he saw Patrick and a young woman walk through the door.

After the barmaid had delivered two beers to their table, Wayne walked over, pulled a chair up and joined them. Patrick flinched and went slack-jawed in surprise. His companion, who appeared to be a carry-over flower-child from the sixties, looked at Wayne as if he were an unwelcome intruder.

Wayne returned her glare, then said: "Honey, why don't you go to the ladies room and powder your nose?"

"Well," she said haltingly. "I don't use face powder and I don't have to go. An' anyway," she snapped as she regained her composure, "you don't. . . ."

"Yes I do," Wayne interrupted her. "Take a walk, honey. Your friend here an' I've got business." She looked imploring at Patrick, who appeared intent on peeling the paper label off a beer bottle. With a derisive snort, she shoved her chair back and headed for the rest rooms.

Wayne turned his attention to Patrick. "You didn't show," he said softly.

"I, uh, I tried to get you the money," the young man stammered. "Dock said he'd help me out, but he had to wait till after the race Sunday, when he'd have some money. I saw him just today. He hasn't got his winnings yet. Something about checking out the horses, or something. Uh, you know, they check for drugs an' stuff, you know. Anyway, we'll have the money for sure in a day or two."

"I know," Wayne drawled, with a look of aversion. "I'm gonna leave your lady friend cab fare and you're coming with me. We've got business to talk over."

"I don't want to go anywhere," Patrick argued. "Just got here, an' anyway, I got friends here that'll be coming over pretty soon to see what's goin' on."

Wayne pushed his chair back and stood up. He pulled a twenty dollar bill from his pocket and set it under the girl's beer bottle and then took Patrick by the arm. "Come on shit-for-brains," he said. "I wouldn't want to drag your ass out of here, in front of all your friends. You won't get hurt if you play the game."

The letter came on Saturday. It was on fancy, sky-blue stationary and addressed in feminine handwriting. There was no return address. It was postmarked in El Paso, Texas.

With a mixed feeling of hesitancy and excitement, Sonny took his pocket knife and slit the top of the envelope. He slipped out two folded perfumed pages and opened them. Still no return address, only the heading "Friday". The letter read:

Dear Sonny,
I was thrilled and so excited while I watched the race. And when I

saw you sitting, so proud, on your Paragon of Merit in the winner's circle, I cried. I just knew you could do it. In fact, I bet twenty dollars on you to win. Ha!

Sonny, I know you must hate me, and maybe you are not even bothering to read this. It is important that you do. I want to try and explain my actions, and I want to warn you and your friends. I was to be paid if I could get you to throw the race. I was told to do whatever it took to get you to agree, and you'd get a big payoff. It sounded like easy money for both of us, and as I didn't know you, it seemed OK. I'm a party girl, and entertaining men is my way of making a living. But you messed me up, especially when you sent me those roses. You're not like the other men I've known. I knew you wouldn't sell out Dock and J.P., and I told them that. But they wouldn't listen, so, the only thing for me to do was to make you mad so you would leave me alone.

Then I ran. Sonny, be careful. Tell Dock and J.P. to watch out. I can't mention any names, and I want you to burn this letter, and please don't tell anyone who gave you the warning. I'm afraid. If you need to get in touch, Barbara is still in Sierra Vista.

Love,

C

25

The phone call came on
Monday, shortly before noon. They paged Dock from the office, over the loud speaker that carried messages to the barn area. He took the call on a backside pay phone in a breezeway of the barn which housed Paragon's stall.

"Is this Dock Trainham?" the caller asked.

"Yeah, what's left of him," Dock bantered. "What can I do for you?"

"You've entered a horse named Paragon of Merit in the trial runs for the Rainbow Futurity?"

"Yes I have."

"There is a question concerning the identity of the horse when we compare its papers with the registration papers filed with the Quarter Horse Association on a stallion named Paragon of Merit."

"Who am I talking to?" Dock asked, the congeniality of a few seconds ago gone from his voice.

"This is the Racing Commissioner's Office in El Paso," the woman stated. "We need to be certain the horse you've registered with the Association and the horse you intend to run are one and the same."

"It's the same horse," Dock replied. "I registered Paragon of Merit with the Association as a yearling and the horse in the trial run is a two year old. Same damned horse, markings are all the same. I don't see where there can be any mix-up."

"What you'll have to do," the caller said, "is to have the track vet take a print of the chestnuts on the horse you'll run so we can compare them with the chestnuts on the registered Paragon of Merit. We need that first thing in the morning, Mister Trainham."

"Well, hell!" Dock stormed. "Say, who am I talking to?"

But the caller had hung up. Dock slammed the receiver onto its bracket and stomped back to the stall, muttering to himself about bureaucrats, ineptness and red tape.

"I can't imagine what the hell's going on," Dock grumbled to J.P.

"Well," J.P. drawled, "if they think there might be two horses involved, comparing the prints will straighten it out. Chestnuts on horses are like fingerprints on people, you know. They're different on every horse."

"I know that'll straighten it out," Dock said, "but it means a trip to El Paso and there shouldn't be any mix-up. I filled out both sets of papers and the information on both was the same except for the age. It's all a bunch of stupid bull shit," he stormed.

"I'll get the track vet over here an' we'll take the prints," J.P. said. "Then, why not kill two birds with one stone. You know, I mentioned using your pickup to go to El Paso and get Virginia and Lynn. What would you think of me taking your pickup, carrying the papers to the Commissioner and bringing my family an' their belongings back? You could use my car while I'm gone."

"That'd be find," Dock agreed. "Save me a trip."

"I'll tell you what else I'd like to do if it's OK with you," J.P. said. "I'd like to stay overnight in El Paso. Come back sometime the next day. Robert'll be here to help with the horse. I'd like to treat my wife and daughter to a night in the swankiest hotel in town," J.P. continued with a wistful smile on his face. "Maybe go to Juarez for dinner. Then I'd like to take them on a shopping spree. I know Virginia's sure not had much money to spend on clothes an' such."

"J.P.," Dock said, "you go and don't you show your face around this barn until after you've entertained those two girls royally. I'll see you after you've moved 'em here and they're set up for housekeeping. Robert an' I can handle things. After all, there's nothing to do but sit around and wait for the trial runs."

"That'd be great," J.P. said, a wide grin fracturing his ruddy, Irish face. "You don't know how I'm looking forward to having my girls back. Having a family again, somebody waitin' for me when I get home nights, somebody to share. Man, that'll be living again, and I can hardly wait."

"I know," Dock said as he slowly nodded his head.

J.P. saw the shadow of longing sadden Dock's features. "I'll tend to things here today and plan on leaving early in the morning," he said, changing the subject. "I'll meet you for breakfast at five thirty an' we'll exchange vehicles. Okay?"

"That'll be fine," Dock agreed.

Later, when Dock went to his room after lunch for his siesta he noticed the message light on the phone was lit. The desk clerk gave him a number to call, a local number Dock did not recognize. He dialed and a woman with an Hispanic accent answered: "Hello."

"This is Dock Trainham, I had a call from this number."

"Just a minute, pleeze," she responded. A few moments elapsed during which Dock could hear muted conversation in the background. He heard someone pick up the receiver. "Mister Trainham," a husky voice said, "This is Vince Scavarda."

Dock tensed. "Yes?" he questioned.

"Trainham, I wanna tell you your horse ran a damned good race yesterday."

"It was a tight race. Maybe we were lucky," Dock said, but thought: Scavarda what the hell's your game now?

"I cashed a win ticket on your horse," Scavarda said, "so I want to buy your dinner tonight. I'll pick you up at your motel at seven thirty."

A congratulatory call and an offer to buy supper was not what Dock expected from Scavarda. Taken flat-footed by the invitation, Dock was caught without a way, short of a flat no, to refuse. "Well, all right. But you don't need to come get me," he replied. "Just tell me where and what time and I'll meet you there. Save you the trouble of coming by here."

"It's no trouble. Meet me in the lobby at seven thirty," Scavarda said and hung up.

"You overbearing son-of-a-bitch!" Dock growled into the dead phone.

Dock looked up from reading the newspaper to see Scavarda come through the double doors into the lobby. He glanced at his wrist watch. I'll be damned, he said to himself, he's on time. They met in front of the registration counter and exchanged hellos. Scavarda had parked in a space reserved for the handicapped.

He drove them up a narrow, wooded canyon to a restaurant set back from the road in a clearing surrounded by towering pines. The building was styled

145

and the decor was that of a Swiss chalet. Scavarda spoke to the hostess, she looked on her reservation sheet and led them to a private dining room. A waiter came to take drink orders. "I want a Royale and seven," Scavarda told the young man, "and I believe my friend drinks Jack Daniels, Black Label, with water."

Surprised, then recollecting the unexplained bottle of Jack Daniels J.P. found in their feed bin, Dock asked: "How do you know what I drink?"

"Mister Trainham," Scavarda started his reply, then injected: "Let's don't be so damned formal. You call me Vince and I'll call you Dock. You ask how I know what you drink. When I deal with people, I make it my business to know everything there is to know about 'em. I know where they're strong and where they're weak. For me, figuring people is like reading a book. What you see on the cover doesn't tell you much about what's inside. You have to read the book. Same way with people. I make sure I know what's between the covers. That's how I happen to know you drink Jack Daniels, Black Label."

To know is to be forewarned, Dock said to himself.

Over their drinks and during the meal they talked on general matters at the track and about the weather. The waiter cleared the soiled dishes off the table and refilled the coffee cups. Scavarda offered Dock a cigar, which to Dock's surprise, he accepted.

Scavarda leaned back in his chair, looking at Dock through the bluish gray smoke from the freshly lit cigars. "Dock," he said, "my wife, may her soul rest in peace, used to tell me I was bullheaded. Well, she was right. And people will tell you I'm a hard man to deal with. Well, they're right. I didn't work my way from being a poor slob on the dock to a man who owns a fleet of tankers by being a pushover. When I'm on a deal I make sure I've got the ways and means to give me the advantage. Now you know I want to buy that black horse of yours. I've made an offer, and you turned it down. OK, tell me what you gotta have for it."

They sat in silence, seemingly engrossed in savoring the richness of the cigars, but each taking the measure of his adversary across the linen-covered table. Dock had known all along that the pitch was coming, but nevertheless he had enjoyed the prime rib dinner while he waited. He leaned back in his chair, took the cigar from his mouth and took pleasure in his reply: "Vince, I enjoyed the supper. I appreciate it, even though, as you said, it was winnings from my horse that paid for it. And I can appreciate you wanting to own Paragon. But Vince, I don't appreciate your underhanded ways."

146

Dock leaned into the table, puffed for a long moment on the cigar then continued: "I'll tell you again, Vince, the horse isn't for sale. In this case, Scavarda, you don't have the ways or the means to get what you want, so call your damned dogs off. I've had a bellyful of your shenanigans."

Scavarda idly rotated the cigar held in his pursed lips. His eyes narrowed in a scowl. After a long studied pause, he took the cigar from his mouth and said with deliberation: "Trainham, I could do big things with that horse, because I've got the money and the connections. Things you can't begin to do. You'll dick around these hick tracks until the horse is just another also-ran. But I'll be goddamned if I can do business with a man as unreasonable as you are. If you're smart you'd take your winnings and what I'd pay for the horse and go the hell back to your ranch, where maybe you know what the fuck you're doing."

As Dock crushed out the cigar in the ash tray he said: "Scavarda, your wife had you pegged right. Take your money and stick it up your ass." He pushed his chair back, turned and walked out of the room. "I knew I should've brought my pickup," he grumbled as he dug into his pocket for a quarter to put in the pay phone.

26

They met for breakfast at the Dew Drop Inn, an all-night greasy-spoon cafe which catered to truckers and track employees.

"You could float a number two horseshoe in this coffee," Dock said with a grimace as he sipped on the black brew which smelled and tasted like it had been simmering in the pot for hours. "Two cups of this an' I'll have a case of the Arbuckle thumps."

"You're right," J.P. said "this stuff's stout enough to float a horseshoe."

"Here are the registration and nomination papers, the report from the vet and my pickup keys," Dock said as he laid an envelope and a ring of keys on the table. "If you run into trouble, call me. I'll be around the backside."

"Okay," J.P. said, "and here's my car keys. If you need me, here's the phone number at the cafe where Virginia works. You can call and leave a message. I'll check there from time to time."

The page came over the loud speaker as Dock and Robert were getting ready to put Paragon on the walker: "Dock Trainham. Telephone call. Pick it up on the pay phone at Barn F."

As he walked to the breezeway and the phone, Dock puzzled over who would want him, and why. J.P. hadn't been gone long enough to be in El Paso.

The phone was ringing as he got to it. He picked up the receiver and said: "This is Dock Trainham."

"Mister Trainham, this is the State Police Dispatcher," a woman's voice said. "We show you as the registered owner of a nineteen eighty four Ford pickup with Texas license TP 874. Is this correct?"

"Yeah," Dock replied, his body tensing and his mind racing over probable cause.

"Mister Trainham," the dispatcher continued, "your pickup was found about an hour ago on the south side of Apache Summit. Apparently the vehicle, traveling at a high rate of speed, failed to make a tight curve, went through the guard rail and rolled to the bottom of a deep canyon. The preliminary examination by the investigating officer shows only one person involved. He has been identified as J.P. Bates of Sierra Vista."

"How bad's he hurt?" Dock blurted out.

"They've taken him to the hospital in Sierra Vista."

"He works for me. He was driving my pickup to El Paso," Dock told the lady. "What caused the accident?"

"The report radioed in stated there were no indications on the pavement of emergency braking where the vehicle crashed through the guard rail. It could have been a malfunction of the vehicle, the driver could have fallen asleep or another vehicle could have crowded it off the road. The officer is still at the scene."

Dock thanked the woman and hung up the phone. Back at the walker he instructed Robert to put Paragon back in the stall and stay with him. He sped to the hospital. J.P. was in the emergency room. The nurse in the corridor would only tell Dock that the patient was listed as critical. Dock left and headed south up the mountain toward Apache Summit. A mile or so beyond the summit he found a State Police cruiser and a wrecker parked by the side of the highway.

The State Policeman, who stood beside Dock as they watched the wrecker winch the pickup up out of the deep, almost vertically-sided canyon, commented: "It's a wonder your friend survived. It totaled the vehicle. I haven't yet figured how come he went off the road without any sign of trying to brake or correct. Judging by the force it would take to break through the guard rail, he had to be really movin' on, otherwise that heavy rail would have deflected the pickup and kept it from going over."

Robert told Dock the word going around the backside was that J.P.'s accident was probably a DWI case. Dock scowled and retorted: "That's a bunch of malarkey, Robert. I had breakfast with J.P. just before he left. If he'd been drinking, I would have smelled it on him. The police don't know yet what caused him to go over the side, but I'm gonna try and find out."

Dock called the Racing Commissioner's office in El Paso to explain why he had not delivered the requested papers. No one there could understand why he was calling. They had no problem with Paragon of Merit's registration and nomination.

The mechanic Dock hired to study what was left of the pickup told him the brake fluid, under the pressure of braking on the six percent grade off Apache Summit, had been forced through a small puncture in the hydraulic hose, a hole that could have been made with a knife or an ice pick. He also found the tie rod connecting the steering mechanism to the front wheels had been partially cut through, marked like it might have been done with a hacksaw blade. The tie rod had given away under the pressure of forceful steering as J.P. attempted to make the hairpin curve at high speed.

With blood in his eye, Dock sped up the winding canyon road to Vince Scavarda's residence. The Mexican housekeeper answered the door chimes and, at Dock's request, led him to the study where the man he was looking for was watching the evening news.

The look on Scavarda's face when he looked over to see Dock striding across the room was evident that Dock was the last person he expected to see. Dock stood looking down at the man reared back in the reclining chair. The blood pounded at Dock's temples and he unconsciously clenched and unclenched his fists in frustrated anger.

It was Scavarda who spoke first: "You wanna see me, Trainham?"

"You sorry bastard," Dock said through gritted teeth and shook his head like a bull on the fight. "Get up out of that chair an' take those glasses off. I'm gonna kick the livin' shit out of you!"

Scavarda did not move. "You got a long fuse, Trainham, or did it take you this long to get enough guts to come jump me?"

"You set it up to get me killed, you son-of-a-bitch. You missed me, but you got J.P."

Scavarda scowled at Dock, studied for a moment then said: "I heard about it. You accusin' me of having something to do with your trainer gettin' drunk an' running off the mountain?"

"You know damned well it wasn't caused by drinking and you know damned well it was no accident!" Dock exclaimed. "And the call that was supposed to be from the Racing Commissioner ordering me to go to El Paso. You set that call up. Then you had me leave my pickup at the motel last night when you took me to supper. Time for your muscle boys to booby trap it so it'd go off the mountain. You figured to get me out of the way so you could get your hands on that horse. Because you can't stand to have someone buck you, a man's fighting for his life.

"Get up from that chair Scavarda. Stand up you sorry bastard or I'll drag your ass out of there."

Scavarda did not move. He looked beyond Dock, his eyes narrowed. After long, emotion-bristling moments he said in a moderate voice: "Trainham, you pissed me off when you turned down my first offer to buy your horse. You needed money. I knew you did, but you were too damned independent to take my offer."

"Get up!" Dock growled through clenched teeth.

"Sit down Trainham, and listen to what I've got to say. When I get done, and if you still want it, I'll give you all the satisfaction you can handle."

Dock did not move from where he stood beside the recliner. Scavarda continued: "Yeah, I worked the angles trying to push you into accepting my offer. That's just good business tactics. I had a bug put on your phone. You thought you were so damned smart catchin' on. Shit, Trainham, I wanted you to know it. I wanted you to feel the pressure. Believe me, if I had wanted it the other way, you'd a never known what the hell was going on. Yeah, the boys put the Jack Daniels in your feed box then planted the rumor so your trainer'd think you sold out on him. I brought a hooker in to lay your jockey and sweet talk him into accepting a payoff and throw the Oklahoma race. Huh!, that backfired," Scavarda snorted. "The girl chickened out. Now the boys tell me she's left the hutch and is selling women's clothes in a fancy store in El Paso.

"I knew your weaknesses, Trainham. If you would have fired your trainer for drinking or if you wouldn't a won the Oklahoma you would've taken a different view of my offer. I figured to drive wedges in the cracks so you'd decide the easy way would be to sell out and go home. But let me tell you something. I don't want, or need your fuckin' horse bad enough to resort to the rough stuff. I don't have to do that anymore. My money talks for me now. Trainham, I had nothing to do with your pickup going off the road, and I'm sorry about your trainer. But maybe I know who wants you out of the way. You give me a few days, I'll put out a little bait an' I think our rat will come out of his hole. I'll let you know if it works. Now, how about a double Jack Daniels to calm you down?"

27

"You know I've never been one to use seat belts; always thought they were a darn nuisance," J.P. said to Dock, Virginia and Lynn standing around his hospital bed. "But that morning, when I got in the pickup, something prompted me to cinch myself up. Maybe it was because I wasn't used to driving your truck, Dock, maybe it was, well, I don't know, but thanks be to the good Lord I did. The cop who pulled me out of the wreck told me that being buckled in probably saved my life. It kept me from being thrown out and crushed or going through the windshield when we hit bottom. I've ridden the hurricane deck on some rank horses and bulls that shook me up pretty bad, but I'll tell you the ride down the side of that canyon, over the boulders and through the trees, was a wild booger bear."

"The patrolman said he figured you hit the dash with your head causing the concussion and the steering wheel column crushed your chest," Dock said. "I don't know how you survived. The truck looks like a wadded-up beer can."

"I don't know what happened," J.P. puzzled. "Everything was fine, it was just breaking day when I topped over Apache Summit and started down the other side. I eased onto the brakes to kind of slow down some. Then, about halfway down, where the grade really gets steep, I noticed the pedal was beginning to get soft. Pretty quick it just went clean to the floor, no brakes and a runaway truck. I never even thought about the emergency brake, I was too busy bracing to make the turn around the next curve. Would you believe it, I'm steering for all I'm worth when all of sudden the steering wheel just goes limp in my hands. It was Katy-bar-the-door, there was no steering, just like riding a crazy runaway horse without any reins. Next thing I knew we crashed through the guard rail and sailed out over the rim of the canyon. She got her head down between her front legs and we went to cartwheeling. That must have been when I hit my head, 'cause I don't remember the rest of the ride."

"I guess my old pickup was just worn out. Too many miles over rough pastures caused mechanical failure," Dock lied.

Freckle-faced Lynn, with her auburn hair tied in a pony tail, was delighted at Dock's offer to put her on the payroll as a helper for Robert. Dock was pleased to note that, as J.P. had said, the teenager was a natural with horses and a welcome ray of sunshine around the barn.

Paragon ran a good race in the trial run and qualified as a contender for the pot of gold at the end of the Rainbow Futurity. That this unknown stallion with singular breeding from an obscure stable in the outback of west Texas stood a chance of winning the Triple Crown created a wave of intense interest in racing circles. Dock was besieged by sports writers wanting Paragon's story, opportunists offering him sure-fire, money-making ways to invest his winnings, general well-wishers and the curious. It seemed like someone was always waiting to waylay him in the motel lobby or at the barn. And he dreaded hearing the phone ring.

He switched off the light on the night stand and lay staring into the darkness, thinking about tomorrow and the last futurity. We've come a long way with your colt, Martha, and I should be on cloud nine, but I'm not, he thought. Maybe it's because you're not here to share it with me. I know one thing for sure, I'm tired of town life, tired of camping in a motel and eating in a cafe. And I'm tired of the track. This style of life is all right for some, but it's not for me. Win, lose or draw tomorrow, I'm ready to hang it up and go home.

The ten horses broke clean, head to head, from the starting gate. At the halfway marker on the four hundred and forty yard sprint, Paragon and Hallelujah had pulled ahead by half a length. The track announcer's calling was almost drowned out by the shouts from the spectators. Paragon of Merit and Hallelujah, their necks stretched out, their ears laid back, their digging hooves throwing clods of track turf behind them, were closing on the finish line in a dead heat. Both jockeys, lying horizonal over the withers, were laying on their bats, pushing their straining mounts to give one last surge of speed.

The bettors went wild. They were on their feet, shouting, jumping, waving their arms to urge on their pick of the field. The ten horses, hardly more than a length distance between the leaders and the trailers, thundered across the finish line.

"A photo finish!" boomed the voice of the announcer.

The uproar almost hushed as the crowd quieted in anticipation, waiting for the official declaration. The tension and suspense that had been building ever since the day Dock had loaded Paragon in the stock trailer at the ranch and set off for Sierra Vista had peaked in these last twenty-one seconds. A crackle on the public address system, then: "Ladies and gentlemen, the official results of the twenty-first running of the Rainbow Futurity: Winner by a nose, Hallelujah, owned by Okeechobee Stables of Clewiston, Florida, trained by Victor Smith and ridden by Art LeBlanc. In second place, Paragon of Merit. . ."

The nervous strain that had gripped Dock since early morning and climaxed in the last few seconds, faded, leaving him drained and weak in the knees. There were no feelings of disappointment, wishing for a different outcome or regrets. Only the lifting of a great weight off his shoulders. Paragon and Sonny had run a good race. They had given it their best. He left the viewing stand with Robert and Lynn and headed for the paddock.

What started as a pipe dream for Dock had been borne on the winds of Fortune and a Paragon of Merit to a reality far beyond the wildest expectations.

Driving along the winding, roller-coaster streets of the village on the way to pick up Virginia at the house she had rented, Dock mused over the events of the summer. Hard to believe, he thought, that putting Martha's colt on the track would turn out like it did, that just a horse could turn so many people's lives around.

The telephone call earlier that afternoon summoning Dock to Scavarda's, the surprise at finding Ross and Patrick there, and the lengthy, sometimes heated, arbitration that had filled in the blanks and tied up the loose ends for Dock had enabled him to make decisions and plan the immediate future.

He picked up Virginia and drove to the hospital.

"You know," J.P. said, "Hallelujah was fresh out of Florida when he ran against us in the Oklahoma. It takes time for a horse coming from sea level to perform at its best in this high altitude with its thin air. In the time between the two races, Hallelujah musta got acclimated. I kinda figured he'd be the horse to beat, but Dock, your horse ran a helluva race. He's all we've figured him to be, and he's got it all ahead of him."

"That brings me around to what I want to talk to you about," Dock said. "You know about the pressures I've been under from people wanting to buy Paragon and you know something about the people involved. What you don't know is that the call I supposedly got from the Racing Commissioner's Office was a phony, and that your accident was no accident. It was figured that I'd carry the papers over the mountain to El Paso, so my pickup was booby trapped the night before you left. I was the object, not you."

"I'll be damned," J.P. exclaimed. "Scavarda an' his boys play kinda rough, don't they?"

"Well, that's the way I had it figured, so I went up to his place after your wreck an' I jumped him out. He admitted to most of the other shenanigans but he denied having anything to do with the call, or the wreck. He told me he knew some things that I didn't, and that he had a good idea who might have set me up with the bogus call, then rigged the pickup."

"Well I'll be damned," J.P. muttered.

"So, this afternoon, I got a call from Scavarda. He wanted me to meet him at his place. When I got there I noticed Ross's pickup parked in the driveway. And sure enough, Ross was there. And so was my son, Patrick.

"Ross and Patrick were sure surprised when I showed up. As I learned, Ross had been in touch with Scavarda, telling him that he had a deal working whereby he'd have control of Paragon and would consider selling the horse. So after that night when Scavarda took me to supper and I still refused to sell, he set up a meeting with Ross to discuss how Ross figured to get hold of Paragon, and what kind of a deal they might make on the horse."

"Ross?" J.P. puzzled. "Well, that figures. There's something I don't think you know. Ross came to me, claiming that he and some silent partners were going to syndicate Paragon. He wanted me to thrown in with 'em. Wanted me to suggest a price for Paragon to you, a price that they were willing to pay. I told him Paragon wasn't for sale. And that I damned sure wasn't. I guess he figured to somehow get possession of the horse and then sell it to Scavarda."

"Well," Dock said, "the second chapter to that story is that Ross ran into Wayne, your gambler friend. They got to chewing the fat about how the talk was that Scavarda was offering some big money for Paragon. Wayne was needing money, and Ross had some backing. So they put their heads together. They knew that if I wouldn't sell at Scavarda's offer, they sure as hell couldn't come up with enough money to buy the horse and then sell it to Scavarda for a profit. They also knew that Patrick was my only heir. With me out of the way, they would be dealing with Patrick. Patrick owed Wayne a big debt, which he couldn't possibly pay. So Ross offered a deal. If Wayne would sign over Patrick's IOU's to Ross, Ross would agree to not only collect the money but would give Wayne a ten percent bonus for the use of the notes. Ross had it figured how he could use the debt as a leverage over Patrick. Ross put the squeeze on Patrick to pay, threatening him. Patrick was caught between a rock and a hard place. Ross and Wayne were both putting the pressure on and Patrick was afraid of both of them. He tried to buy some time by telling them that he was going to hire a lawyer and go to court to break his mother's will, so he could collect on his inheritance. Ross had made some inquires and he knew the terms of Martha's will. He told Patrick there was no way a court would override Martha's wishes. He planted the idea in Patrick's mind that the only way he'd get any part of his mother's money before the terms of the will were fulfilled was for me to be out of the picture."

"Son of a gun," J.P. said after a little whistle of astonishment. "All over a horse."

"Yep," Dock agreed. "All over a horse, and money."

"So Ross was the one who masterminded the scheme?" J.P. deduced.

"Yeah, and then in order to implicate Patrick he told him to make that bogus call from the Commissioner."

"Didn't you say it was a woman who called?" J.P. questioned.

"It was. Patrick knew I'd recognize his voice so he had his girl friend do it. Ross hired a wet-back to booby trap the truck. Then when he paid him off, he told him that if he didn't hightail it back to Mexico he'd turn him in to the Immigration people."

"Then Scavarda and his boys didn't figure in it at all," J.P. surmised.

"Well, not in the scheme to get me killed, except as the source of a payoff for Ross after I was gone and Ross had bullied Patrick out of the horse."

"So what are you going to do?" J.P. asked.

"I'll tell you what I'm gonna do. I'm going home."

"Oh?" J.P. questioned and glanced at Virginia sitting in a chair by the side of the bed.

"Scavarda and I have buried the hatchet. He told me he'd go along if I wanted to press charges against Ross for attempted homicide," Dock said. "But if I did that, Patrick would be an accessory. So I made a deal with Ross. I agreed not to press charges if he would acknowledge, in a notarized state-ment, his actions and that he would pay all your medical bills that our insur-

156

ance doesn't cover, and remain responsible to compensate you should you suffer any permanent disability. If there is a disability, you two would agree on the insurance company's claim adjuster to assess the damages and the compensation. Then, I've drawn up papers giving you and Virginia, as joint owners, one-half interest in Paragon."

"A half interest in Paragon!" J.P. exclaimed. "Dock, you don't owe us that. I've just got a cracked head, a few broken bones and some bruises. They'll heal. Hell, I've had rodeo bulls mess me up worse than this and as you know, all I got then was some applause from the crowd."

"I'm not compensating you for the wreck," Dock said. "I sure feel bad that the trap caught you, but if I'd a been driving, Ross's plan would probably have worked. I never use a seat belt. I'd been thrown out and the truck would've rolled over me, for sure. My decision was twofold. It was you who brought out Paragon's abilities. Secondly, I'm looking out for myself. I want to go home. I don't want to be tied to a horse on the track. I'll go back to my saddle horses and my cattle. You, Virginia and Lynn can do the worrying over Paragon for all of us.

"There's another chapter to the story and I hope you'll agree with my decision. I've given Scavarda the right to stand Paragon at his farm in New Jersey. He'll pick the horse up in November and bring him back to you in February. He has agreed to share the insurance on Paragon and pay all the expenses while he has him. In exchange, he'll have full breeding rights to his mares. We'll get one-quarter and he'll keep three-quarters of the outside breeding fees. You and Marvin will work out the details. You see, J.P., if it hadn't been for Scavarda, I'd a never known what had happened; and too, he's got the money to promote the horse and the facilities for a first-class stud farm."

"I like Marvin and we can sure get along," J.P. said.

"You'll be going back to the ranch?" Virginia asked.

"Yep," Dock replied as he stood up and reached for his hat. "Patrick and I are going back together. We've agreed that for his mother's memory we've got some rifts to bridge and some fences to mend."

"Oh, and by the way, Sonny called me to say that he would be out of pocket for a few days. Seems like he's got some important personal business to take care of in El Paso."